The Direction You Go

A Novel

by

Robert L. Glass (signature)

Robert L. Glass

ISBN 978-1-66781-327-1
eISBN 978-1-66781-328-8

Printed in the United States of America

For Karen
with love
Her support and help
were amazing

On the Road

The phone rang at 2:15 a.m. Bad news. Brad jumped out of bed and went quickly to answer it. It would be bad news. Only bad news woke you up. Good news waited until after nine in the morning. His roommate Jerry had not come home last night. Jerry's mother was on the phone. Between crying and blowing her nose she managed to say car accident, hospital, and Wisconsin. Hospital, at least he was still alive. Five minutes later Brad went back to bed. He would pick her up tomorrow morning and they would go together to see Jerry. Brad didn't sleep any more that night. The bad news had taken control of his thoughts.

Before leaving to pick up Mrs. Goddard, Brad called his supervisor and left the message he would get to work sometime early in the afternoon. After Mrs. Goddard was seated in the front passenger seat with her seat belt on, they both yawned wide-open mouth yawns at the same time. That caused them both to laugh and broke the tension they had been feeling. They drove north almost in silence. Each was deep in personal thoughts, memories mixed with hopes which were quickly drowned with fears. What conversation did take place was mostly Brad trying to encourage Jerry's mom, "I believe he'll be all right," and "I am sure he'll be all right." They drove straight to the hospital without any stops.

Fairly quickly they made their way to his room located at the far end of the second floor. Hospital smells, smells of

1

sickness and the medicines which were fighting the sicknesses were all about them as they walked quickly to his room and waited for the nurse to invite them in. Jerry lay on his back drugged and not able to talk. The ubiquitous bag of medication hung from the pole on wheels and medicine flowed through the tube and the needle taped to the back of his left hand and into his vein. When his eyes were open he appeared to recognize them and seemed pleased to see them. Jerry's doctor came into the room ten minutes after they were seated by his bed. The doctor told them Jerry's right leg was badly broken and they had set it with two small metal rods which would be permanent, but he would certainly walk again and eventually without a limp. The airbag in his car had deployed and probably saved his life. It left the rest of his body badly bruised with some abrasions and small minor burns which were caused by the airbag itself. He could be expected to leave the hospital in about two weeks. The hospital preferred to err on the side of caution and not release him early with any remaining issues, especially head injuries which required time to ensure proper recovery. Brad and Mrs. Goddard were only allowed to remain with him for fifteen minutes that first day, but they left feeling ever so much better knowing he would be home in two weeks.

When Brad arrived at work, he arranged to leave early the next two Tuesdays and Thursdays in order to make the long drive up to Oconomowoc, Wisconsin, and for longer if Jerry remained in the hospital longer. Over the next two weeks they visited him on those two days. On Saturdays Brad drove alone so he and Jerry could say things they didn't want Mrs.

2

Goddard to hear. They created a plan to have Brad pick up Jerry when he was released and to drive him somewhere at least one hundred miles away from home so his mother would not interfere with his recovery. After several possible destinations were discussed, Brad chose Piggott, Arkansas, home of the Hemingway-Pfeiffer Museum. He wanted to see the barn where the better part of *A Farewell to Arms* had been written.

Two weeks after the first visit, Brad learned that Jerry was to be released from the hospital at 11 a.m. the following Monday. Back home he finished packing the four suitcases, two for him and two for Jerry. He went over the list several times to reduce the chance something needed would have been left behind. Sunday evening, he went to bed early but found it was difficult to fall asleep while plans for their trip entered and left and reentered his head.

His alarm went off before 6 a.m. and when it did, he got up quickly. He dressed, ate breakfast, washed, and put away the dishes, searched his mind for anything he might have forgotten, and locked the front door behind him. The final chore on his to do list was to drop off his house keys with his parents so his sister could pick them up when she arrived in town. On Friday he had stopped at his bank to get enough cash for the trip and to inform them his charge card would now show purchases in Arkansas for the next six months.

Driving up the now familiar roads to Oconomowoc he thought about what to say to Jerry and what to avoid saying.

He worried about how long Jerry could sit in the car and how long to plan for rest stops. Probably it would be best to let Jerry decide those things. He arrived at the hospital ten minutes before the eleven o'clock release time, parked, and went inside. He waited by the receptionist for more than thirty-five minutes as she kept assuring him Jerry would be there in just a few minutes. He had asked her what her name was and found out it was Becky, but people kept coming by so he couldn't have much of a conversation with her. He did manage to ask her four times, "Becky, could you find out when Jerry will get here?"

Finally, the orderlies arrived pushing Jerry in a wheelchair. They told Brad to pull up to the door and they would help Jerry into the car. Brad hurried to the car, drove up the circular drive and stopped with his front passenger door in line with the hospital door. The sun was shining, the temperature was pleasant, and a soft breeze was detectable. Soon the two orderlies had Jerry out of the wheelchair and in the passenger seat of Brad's silver-gray two-year-old Volkswagen. It almost seemed like a comedy of errors as they started to put in one leg, backed out and tried to put in two legs, backed out again and managed to put in one leg at a time. They helped him put on his seat belt, put the crutches he would use on the back seat, handed the bag of his personal items to Brad, wished them a safe trip back to Illinois, and quickly vanished behind the hospital double doors.

When they could no longer hear him, Brad said, "Goodbye Mr. Hope and Mr. Crosby." As he walked around the back of the car the realization of what he was doing made him miss a step and he nearly fell flat on his face. Quickly on the heels of that realization came another. No matter what it took out of him, he had to keep Jerry's spirits up. This was the greatest challenge he had ever faced, but it could also be the most rewarding thing he had ever done. He silently said a quick prayer to the god he wasn't sure he knew, "God help me succeed and bring my best friend Jerry back to me. You know, the one who loved life and laughed and sang and drank with me." He climbed into the driver's seat and bumped his left knee on the steering wheel.

"Hey Jerry, did you catch that receptionist?" he asked.
Jerry just looked out the window as Brad drove away from the hospital and out into traffic. Slowly a sort of smile came onto Jerry's recently shaven face.
"Is that why you came to see me so often?"
"Hell no. Becky was really attractive. The afternoon desk lady looks like J. Edgar Hoover in curls. If Becky had been there, I might have never made it to your room."
Coming to a stop at the first red light, Brad worried about the slight jerking motion and its effect on Jerry. He was just sitting there looking out the window. Brad thought he looked much like the ticket taker at Old Town's long since closed Wax Museum, lifeless but life like.

Normally the drive from Oconomowoc to Piggott, Arkansas could be made in one very long day or two normal driving days, about nine hours driving time, but since Jerry wouldn't be able to sit for long periods of time and needed extra hours of sleep, Brad decided to take three days and allow time for long rests along the way. He also wanted to avoid the high-speed interstate highway. They would allow two hours for lunch each day and find a motel well before dark each night. Once they were out of town and driving without very much traffic, Jerry asked him, "How much vacation were you able to get?"

"Not enough. I decided to ask for a leave of absence for six months."

"I thought your company doesn't grant leaves."

"Normally they don't. My boss told me it couldn't be done. So, I asked him if I should resign to him or to our vice president. He said to talk to the VP. After telling me the company didn't give leaves, we talked about why I needed it and he surprised me by saying he had heard only good things about my work, and he would make this one exception and give me six months leave. Without pay of course."

"Of course."

"So how do we pay for the B&B in Piggott, gas, meals, and the rest?" Jerry inquired. He seemed more alert and interested now than he had been earlier.

"You know I was given some stock by my parents. Each month I bought more shares and each quarter I reinvested the dividends. I just sold thirty shares of 3M and put the money in my checking account. Each quarter I will get additional dividends to replace some of what we have spent. We can almost make it six months on that alone, but I plan to look for a little part-time work after a couple of weeks in Piggott."

"You did all that for me?" Jerry asked after thirty seconds of silence had passed.

"No Jer, I did it for us."

Stopping for lunch, Brad walked around the car, opened
Jerry's door, waited until he was out of the car and on the
crutches which Brad had handed him. Brad then closed and
locked the car door and walked up to the restaurant. At that
point Jerry had advanced about four steps. Brad decided the
best routine was to stand outside the restaurant and read the
menu until Jerry was there. He then opened the restaurant
door and followed Jerry to the table.

Being an animal lover Brad had become a vegetarian about
seven months prior and was enjoying putting together meals
which he could order that had no meat in them. At one
restaurant he had wonderful French onion soup which Jerry
pointed out was made with beef broth. Jerry usually ate a
cheeseburger, a BLT sandwich, or a Reuben. One evening
he had a turkey and mashed potatoes dinner. Bradley always
had hot tea at lunch and a stein of beer at dinner. Following
his doctor's advice Jerry didn't drink yet, but he always took
one sip of the beer when Brad put the stein down.
"Thanks, old buddy for the taste" was always his comment,
and usually a wink of his right eye to show he was aware he
was cheating on the doctor's advice.

The motels they stopped at were not overly expensive, just
one step above economy. They always got a room with two
beds and asked for the handicapped room because the
handicapped bathroom was so much easier for Jerry to use.
The motel they stayed in the second night did not have a

handicapped room and Jerry had lots of problems using the bathroom. Brad heard a dozen or more naughty words said to no one in particular. He did not intervene because Jerry had said he was going to try to do nearly everything on his own beginning with the bathroom that night. He did help Jerry pull on the right leg of his pajamas when Jerry asked him to.

The first day on the road had seemed to last forever with hardly a word spoken.

Brad said a few things like "isn't that tree interesting" or "what a terrible color to paint a barn," but Jerry didn't reply to any such comments. At the long lunch the only conversation was what to order and "I'm going to the restroom." The second day Brad felt he had to get a real conversation going.

"How about the license game? First one with twenty different states wins."

"No thanks," Jerry replied in a bored tone.

"How about the alphabet game? Spot each letter of the alphabet in sequence on road signs only."

"Not today."

"Well then, let's try to say as many different contradictory phrases as we can," Brad said.

"I'll go first. The tall midget smiled through his tears."

Two minutes passed. Then Jerry said, "The fat foolish philosopher farted in public again."

Taking turns, they bounced back and forth quickly without any thinking time.

"The dry rain killed my wilted flowers."

"The young man had several diseases often seen in older women."

"I dropped my fragile cup and it bounced back up."

"The wild animal trap had a bag of children's candy as bait."

"That's kind of mean, man," Brad said, then "The bright red shirt and luminescent pants made him hard to see."

After a few minutes of quiet Brad began again, "The cat barked, and the dog meowed and hissed."

Jerry quickly followed with, "The short cane helped him walk bent forward."

"I bet my seven-dollar bill on the lottery and lost sixty bucks on the numbers."

"After years of saving money, I was finally able to buy this candy bar."

"The purple stop sign meant only royals had to stop."

"My rabbit is flat, and my girlfriend hops and stares."

"I fell up the inside stairs and broke the front doorbell at the same time."

"My dog licked my cat, and she gave birth to dogittens."

"Good one," Brad said, then "I fly my plane upside down to see the moon better."

"The short horse walked over the high fence while singing the blues."

"The giving tree repossessed my gifts."

"I never try but they still call me trying."

"My friend drowned in the dry, dry desert."

"My beer tastes like turpentine. It is turpentine."

"The pear I picked from the cherry tree tasted like ginger and rye."

After a few more moments of quiet Jerry asked, "Are we having fun yet?"

Brad's answer was "Absolutely maybe."

That afternoon they again stopped early, still in the beige and green corn and soybean fields of spring in southern Illinois. At dinner Jerry talked more than he had on the trip so far.

"I don't know what I would have done if you hadn't offered to take me south to heal. Mom was crying and practically smothering me each time she came to the hospital. I just couldn't move back with her to heal. In two days, I would have had to ask to go back to the hospital or somewhere else away from her. Ever since her brother died, she has hung over me like a blanket smothering what it was meant to protect."

"I knew that. We are closer than most twins. We agreed on one Saturday conversation to travel at least one hundred miles from mom. Since I had always wanted to visit the Hemingway-Pfeiffer Museum, Piggott was my first choice. Fortunately, when I called the B&B there Mrs. Barnes was delighted to have us stay with her for the entire six months. I look forward to meeting her. She sounded so great on the phone. Southern hospitality here we come."

"Thank you again for that."

"It's okay. You know I would do anything for you that I could as long as it was legal. Or nearly so."

After breakfast the next morning they got on the road minutes before ten o'clock. Brad drove three miles and not hearing a word from Jerry, he started a conversation.

"You know the whole purpose of this trip is to get you healed from your accident."

"Yes."

"You know the best way to heal is to laugh."

"So says Norman Cousins."

"So say I, too. So, for the next few minutes we will tell each other jokes and stories to cause us to laugh."

"You go first."

"Okay," Brad said, "I heard this joke over and over from Jeannie at the Hemingway Birth House."

"I'm listening."

"This man from Oak Park went to Washington, D.C. on business. He finished his business rather quickly and caught a cab back to the airport. They came to a Catholic Church with a sign out front *Hearing confessions today*. He was not in a hurry, it was the right time, and he was about to catch a plane, so he had the cab stop and wait for him. As luck would have it, he went right into the confessional. 'Forgive me father for I have sinned. I came to Washington, D.C. to beat the heck out of my congressman, and I did.' The priest sat silently for a moment and then replied, 'Son, we are here to forgive sins, not public service.'"

Jerry didn't laugh but a small smirk did appear on his face. He then came back with this,

"Two boys were out playing together. One was named Shut Up. The other was named Trouble. Somehow, they got separated on a long hike so Shut Up went to the police and asked for help in finding his friend. 'What is your name' the policeman asked. 'Shut Up,' he replied. Again, the question

11

what is your name? Again, Shut Up. The policeman then asked him 'Are you looking for trouble?' Yes, I am, how did you know?"

"Nice. We told that joke in third grade. Still cute though. Another priest joke. A loyal parishioner was near the confessional when the priest stepped out. Cover for me Bill. I have to go pee. I don't know what to say. There is a chart on the wall. Just find the sin and then read the penance. Off he went so Bill stepped into the booth. The first confession was easy enough. 'Forgive me father for I have sinned. I allowed hate to enter my mind.' From the penance list Bill read, 'Say two Hail Marys, pray the Rosary, and attend mass the next four weeks.' The next one was easy too. 'Forgive me father for I have sinned. I coveted my neighbor's red sports car.' Bill read, 'Your penance is to say five Hail Marys, pray the Rosary three times, and ask God to forgive you.' Then came the stumper. 'Forgive me father for I have sinned. I had anal sex with a teenaged boy.' Not on the list, Bill searched his memory. 'I guess that will cost you two bottles of cola and a chocolate candy bar.'"
Jerry smiled but then laughed out loud as the full meaning of the joke hit him.

Jerry contributed next, "Did you hear about the mathematician who was afraid of negative numbers? He will stop at nothing to avoid them."
Brad laughed a subdued laugh. "Good one. How about we are reading signs at our favorite diner. First one reads 'Good morning let the stress begin,' next one 'Give me coffee now

and no one gets hurt,' next one 'Beer helping ugly people have sex for more than 100 years,' next one 'Just shut up and eat it.' On the other wall. 'After one drink of coffee do stupid things faster with more energy.' Then 'No whining, crying or loud complaining, this is a respectable diner.' Another one 'Variable pricing. Complain to your waitress and the price of your lunch goes up.' Last one 'Today's blue plate special, take it or leave it.'"

Jerry said, "I remember those, seeing as I was always the one with you at the diner."

After a moment he said, "Helvetica and Times New Roman walk into a bar. 'Get out of here!' shouts the bartender. 'We don't serve your type.'"

Brad smiled. "Perfect one for me, the novelist."

"Speaking of which, where is your novel."

"Mostly in my head, but it will go on paper in Piggott while you are getting better."

"Dollar says it won't."

"I'll take that bet if you give me ten thousand words or more is enough for me to win the bet."

"You got it. But I get to read it, so you don't pad it with and and and, by buy by, for for for, me me me, too to two."

Jerry continued, "I have another one for you novel writing friend. Yesterday I saw a guy spill all his Scrabble letters on the road. I asked him, 'What's the word on the street?'"

"Perfect. I actually laughed silently to that one."

Brad began again, "Now some quotes, a member of Parliament to Disraeli 'Sir, you will either die on the gallows or of some unspeakable disease.' 'That depends, Sir' said Disraeli 'On whether I embrace your policies or your mistress.'

Next quote, 'He had delusions of adequacy.' I love that one. Winston Churchill said, 'He has all the virtues I dislike and none of the vices I admire.'

Clarence Darrow said, 'I have never killed a man, but I have read many obituaries with great pleasure.'

Mark Twain similarly said, 'I didn't attend the funeral, but I sent a nice letter saying I approved of it.'

I forgot who, but someone once said, 'Thank you for sending me a copy of your book, I'll waste no time reading it.' Sounds like something I'll hear a few times.

Another someone said, 'I've just learned about his illness. Let's hope it's nothing trivial.'

Oscar Wilde said, 'He has no enemies, but is intensely disliked by his friends.' Hope I never hear that one.

Wilde also said, 'Some cause happiness wherever they go, others, whenever they go.'

George Bernard Shaw sent a note to Winston Churchill which read 'I am enclosing two tickets to the first night of my new play; bring a friend, if you have one.'

Winston Churchill responded, 'Cannot possibly attend first night, will attend second night if there is one.'

Someone once said, 'I feel so miserable without you; it's almost like having you here.'

Also 'He is a self-made man and worships his creator.'

Samuel Johnson said, 'He is not only dull himself; he is the cause of dullness in others.'

And 'He loves nature in spite of what it did to him.'
Mae West said, 'His mother should have thrown him away and kept the stork.'
Billy Wilder said, 'He has Van Gogh's ear for music.'
Groucho Marx said, 'I've had a perfectly wonderful evening. But I'm afraid this wasn't it.'"

Jerry laughed at that one and Brad thought there was the old twinkle in his friend's eyes, but he couldn't look while driving and he was focused on a few more quotes.

He continued, "And again Mark Twain, 'I've lived through some terrible things in my life, some of which actually happened.'

FDR told this story, 'He knew a Republican who took the train into work and when he passed the paper boy he handed him a coin, looked at the front page of the paper and then gave it back to the boy. After three days like that the boy asked him why he did it. He said he was looking for an obituary. The boy told him the obituaries are at the back of the paper, not on page one. 'Not the one I want to see; it will be on the front page' replied the man."

After a minute of silence Brad asked, "So have you laughed enough for one day?"

"It was your idea my friend. I laughed enough after three jokes."

"A smirk is not a laugh, my friend. But you did laugh once or twice that I heard."

Jerry then commented, "And Mae West probably didn't say that. And how do you remember all of those quotes?"

"I planned the laugh fest last night and memorized them while you slept. I had heard them before, so they were fairly easy to memorize."

After a pause Brad said "I just remembered more jokes. Two fish were swimming upstream. Suddenly they hit a wall. Bigger one said 'dam.'"

"Worst one of them all."

"Okay. Why does it help to stand in the corner on a cold day? Because it is always 90 degrees there."

Brad searched his memory and came up with a few more. "Did you hear about the man who quit smoking so he wouldn't die of cancer? He took up chewing on toothpicks and died of Dutch Elm Disease.

I opened my mouth, and my dad came out.

A turtle got mugged by two snails and they got away with everything. When the policeman arrived, he asked if the turtle could give a description of the perpetrators. I can't, he replied, it all happened so fast.

I'll end with Faulkner on Hemingway. 'He has never been known to use a single word that might send the reader to the dictionary.'

And when Hemingway went to Venice after the plane crashes in Africa, 'Another Jungle Bunny heard from.'"

Jerry then confessed, "What really makes me laugh is the movie *Sleeper* by Woody Allen. He runs across a field of tall grass to music like that from the Keystone Cops. He falls, bounces back up. Falls again, bounces up walking sideways. It is slapstick but really funny."

"Then let's picture that together now," Brad said.

16

After telling Brad to keep his focus on his driving, Jerry pictured the scene in his mind and began laughing out loud. "Damn" he said. "Now my head hurts, my lungs hurt, and my right leg hurts. But it was worth it. Laughter is a form of medicine."

Shortly after that they came to a red light and stopped behind a Jeep Wrangler with a soft top. An attractive woman was at the wheel. Brad read the license plate holder 'Sometimes I like to go out topless.' As it dawned on him what that meant he noticed Jerry was almost doubled over with laughter, but he was laughing at him and not at the sign. Jerry knew Brad, at first, was picturing the driver topless.

Piggott

The next morning at breakfast their server was one of those women every man notices. She had shoulder length blond hair, blue eyes that seemed to be winking at you even though they weren't, just the smallest amount of cleavage clearly controlled and not accidental, and long legs beneath a shorter than expected skirt. When she went back in the kitchen Brad whispered to Jerry "That my friend is sex on the hoof."

"Who are you, the bull?"

"No. She isn't my type, but every part of her is as sexy as she could make it."

With a light smile Jerry said, "She dressed for you to notice her, and it worked."

"It always does, doesn't it?"

"I guess. Especially for a horny bastard like you."

"Not horny, just single and alert. I look forward to when you feel good enough to join me in checking out the women."

"That day will come. For now, I am just checking out."

They hadn't been on the road twenty minutes when a car passed them with an oncoming car not very far away. Brad hit the brake hard to let the passing car back in their lane safely. Seeing him safely in front of them only seconds before the oncoming car passed, seemingly not having slowed down at all, Brad said, "May your mother let the air out of your head, may you fly about the room until you're dead, may they place your body down upon the bed, and piss on it."

"Your favorite curse," Jerry said.

"I guess it is. All great curses involve your mother."

"Who were you cursing, the passing driver or the oncoming driver?"

"Both, but mostly the low life who passed when it was unsafe to do so."

"Probably someone late for a meeting."

"Probably a nearsighted jerk who always seems to catch a break."

Clouds were covering the entire sky, but no rain was falling, and none was forecast. Here and there they saw sunshine break through a gap in the clouds in what Jerry called glory holes.

They were supposed to turn left off the main road onto state route ZZ, but by the time Jerry spotted the sign it was too late to turn so Brad pulled off on the right shoulder. When there was no traffic approaching from behind, he backed up until he could back onto the road across from ZZ. Again, when there was no traffic approaching, he crossed two lanes and waited in the middle of the divided highway for a break from their right. On a small break he crossed as quickly as he could.

Jerry inquired, "Do you want to put me back into the hospital?"

"That was safe, and you know it," Brad said a bit sharply. Quickly realizing why Jerry was nervous he added,

"I'll wait for a longer break next time though."

Jerry inquired, "Were you a nearsighted jerk or a low-life?'

Brad looked at him and then they both laughed.

Turning on state road H they were away from all traffic and passing only family farms where recently planted fields were turning green, and no person was seen anywhere. When they came to a one-lane bridge they crossed easily as no other vehicle was on the road.

"Where are you taking me again? Far from the madding crowd I guess."

"True, but I think we will like Piggott. It is just across the border from Missouri in Arkansas. We will be there in less than an hour now."

They crossed a second one-lane bridge but this time they saw an approaching pickup truck which slowed to wait for them to clear the bridge.

They turned left on Missouri route 53 south and looked for Frisco Street. To be certain they had found it Brad pulled into a gas station across from state route OO. A local farmer who was waiting in line to pay for his purchase confirmed OO was Frisco Street. He added they would turn right at the end of OO and drive directly into Piggott. Brad thanked him, joined Jerry in the car, and set off on the final few miles of their trip.

After turning right on US route 62 they saw the sign 'Entering Arkansas' and not long after the sign Piggott 6 miles. The clock on the dashboard read 12:02.

"Let's eat first before we find the B&B," Brad said.

"You're driving. Do as you wish."

Entering Piggott, it seemed to Brad to be just like every other small town. A gas station on each side of the road, small metal buildings housing car repair shops, warehouses, family manufacturing businesses and a Dollar General Store. As they approached downtown, he felt better seeing interesting older buildings. He would have felt terrible if Piggott turned out to be a boring sleepy little town. On one corner there was a two-story brick building which appeared to be a bank. He later learned it was a former bank building used by Paul Pfeiffer, father of Hemingway's second wife Pauline Pfeiffer. Paul had bought the building and used it as his downtown office. That meant Ernest Hemingway had visited his father-in-law in that building dozens of times. Slowly driving in downtown Piggott, they spotted a café on the opposite side of the Courthouse Square. Both said almost in unison "Here" and Brad turned and began looking for a parking spot. Seeing a spot three cars away he stopped, put on the flashers, and went around to open the door for Jerry who was already one foot out of the car when he got there.

"I told you I'll open my own doors from now on."

Brad ignored that comment, opened the back door, picked up the crutches and handed them to Jerry. When Jerry was on the sidewalk before the café Brad got back in the car, parked it in the spot he had seen, locked the car and walked back to the entrance where he entered just behind Jerry.

"Sit anywhere," a voice said. They saw a table for four near the back and sat down there. By the time Jerry was seated a woman about 24 years of age was standing beside the table, order pad in hand. She had shoulder length black hair, hazel eyes which Brad felt were the doorway to a wise soul, a fine symmetrical small mouth without lipstick, and a visible butterfly tattoo on her right leg just below the knee.

22

"You're not from around here," she realized out loud. "The menu is on the blackboard behind the cash register. Specials today are egg salad on rye with homemade chips and coleslaw, country fried chicken with mashed potatoes, and homemade pies cherry, apple, and blueberry." After a short pause she asked, "Where are you from?"

"Chicago," Jerry said.

"Actually, Oak Park, Illinois, birthplace of Ernest Hemingway," Brad corrected him.

"No really? Hemingway lived here with his second wife Pauline Pfeiffer!"

"That is why we are here. I wanted to see the barn where he wrote and the museum here in the Pfeiffer Mansion."

"Do you know much about him?"

"Quite a bit. I was a docent at his birth house for the last nine years. I have given lectures about him at two local clubs including the Nineteenth Century Club where his mother gave lectures on many types of culture when she was a member. I have been up to Petoskey, Michigan for Michigan Hemingway Conferences, attended a conference in Gainesville, Florida where Raul Villarreal asked me to give a talk in place of one speaker who had dropped out, and ..."

"She doesn't need to know all that," Jerry interrupted. "Let's decide what to order."

"I'll give you a few minutes," she said. She turned around and walked back to the cash register where she said something to the older woman standing there. Then they both looked back at the table but quickly looked away as Brad was looking directly at them.

When she returned to the table, they placed their orders. Jerry chose the mushroom cheeseburger with fries. Brad ordered a salad, mashed potatoes and the vegetable of the day which turned out to be peas and carrots. Brad thought that is almost always the vegetable of the day in smaller restaurants.

"I am a vegetarian," he explained.

"Would you like sweet tea with that?"

"Yes please," Brad said.

"No thanks, just water," Jerry said.

When she disappeared through the open doorway with their orders Bradley said in a quiet voice,

"She is very attractive don't you think?"

"The way your eyes followed her, you already told me that. But yes, she is cute, bubbly, and appears to be happy with her job."

Their meals were brought a few minutes later and Bradley asked her,

"Do you know Mrs. Barnes and her B&B?"

"Very well. She is my aunt."

"Is it far from here?"

"Nothing in Piggott is far from here. Are you staying there?"

"Yes, for the next six months."

"Oh, so you are the ones she told me about. What are your names?"

"Bradley."

"Jerry Goddard. Yours?"

"Lynda with a y."

"Great to meet you Lynda with a y. I hope we will see you often while we are staying here."

24

"If you eat here, you will see me five days a week. We are closed on Sundays and Mondays."

"Guess we'll eat somewhere else on those two days."

"I have to get back to work now. Nice to meet you Jerry and Bradley."

Again, as she walked away Bradley's eyes followed her until she disappeared into the back room once again. Obviously, that was where the kitchen was.

When she returned to clear their plates, they ordered dessert. Jerry ordered cherry pie. Bradley ordered blueberry pie. Both ordered black coffee.

As they were getting up to leave, Lynda said, "I will be stopping by to see Aunt Millie tonight. If you feel like it come out of your room and say hello."

"We will do that. Thanks."

"Goodbye and thank you."

Brad left a generous $5 tip on the table and Jerry walked all the way to the car, having refused to wait to be picked up.

When they arrived at Aunt Millie's B&B, Brad parked on the street, and they went inside to check in.

Aunt Millie greeted them as if they were her sons returning from college on spring break. She showed them to their room, a medium-sized room on the first floor with two beds, a couch, a desk, and a dresser. She pointed out the bathroom. Then she asked if they were hungry. Finding out where they had just eaten, she beamed with pride about her niece Lynda. The boys went to their room where Jerry lay down to rest while Brad brought in their luggage. Three trips to the car later, he began to unpack.

"You get the top two drawers and I get the bottom two," he told Jerry.

"You get the right half of the closet and I take the left half. You get the bed closest to the john and I get the one by the wall."

"Capisce."

"Nap time."

"I beat you to bed by twenty-five minutes."

After a fifteen-minute power nap Brad returned to the kitchen where Aunt Millie showed him the refrigerator and told him to help himself as the only meal she prepared for guests was breakfast. He would grocery shop in the morning and stock the refrigerator with dinner items for days when they didn't eat out. That first night they called out for a pizza which was delivered, half onion and mushroom for Brad and half sausage and olives for Jerry. Aunt Millie declined to share their pizza but made a small salad and a small piece of salmon for herself. They all ate together at the table where breakfast would be served each day.

The boys were still at the table with Aunt Millie and were relaxing with coffee when Lynda stopped by. She got a cup of sweet tea and joined the three of them around the kitchen table. She and Aunt Millie talked family for a few minutes and then she turned her attention to Brad,

"So, tell me more. How did you get six months off from work, and what work did you do?"

"I am a computer programmer at a big insurance company in Chicago. When I saw Jerry was in need of rest and recuperation, I asked for six months leave of absence. They had a policy of not granting leaves, but somehow, I got permission to take one from the area VP. He understood how important I was to Jerry, and he liked my work, so he agreed I could come back in six months, and they would find a place for me to work."

"And Piggott because of Ernest Hemingway?"

"Jerry's mother couldn't handle having him move back with her and he did not want to do that either. She is difficult to live with and would have smothered him instead of helping him get back up. We decided we needed miles between her and us and I chose Piggott because Hemingway lived here. I always planned to come here someday anyway. And I promised his mother a phone call at least every two or three days to report on his progress."

"What happened to Jerry?"

"His car went off the road in Wisconsin and hit a tree head on. The passenger side was pushed so far in it would have killed anyone there, but in the driver's seat he was pinned in and badly hurt but alive. Thank God a car was not too far behind him, and they stopped and called for help. The fire department and ambulance arrived in less than twelve minutes, and he was still conscious when they extracted him from his sad old car."

Jerry added, "I guess I dozed off or something and went straight when the road didn't."

Brad continued, "He was in the hospital almost two and a half weeks, so I had plenty of time to make my plans. My sister is looking to buy a townhouse, so she agreed to rent our house for six months by making the mortgage payments for us. That will let her save more for a down payment than she could save if she rented from someone else. My boss let me leave early Tuesdays and Thursdays and I drove up to Oconomowoc where Jerry was in the hospital. Within a couple of weeks our plan came together. Six months of rest with gradual exercise to get Jerry up and running again in a neutral environment away from family and friends. So here we are."

"Speaking of rest, I need to go lie down now," Jerry said. Brad helped him up from the chair and handed him his crutches and he said good night to everyone there and went slowly off into their room. Brad quickly joined him in the room just after he entered it so he could fetch Jerry's pajamas and be there if any further assistance were needed.

Millie said to Lynda "They seem like very nice young men."

"I guess so," she replied.

Jerry is Getting Better

The first two days in Piggott, after eating breakfast, they just stayed in their room until lunch time when they drove the short distance to eat lunch at the café. Lynda waited on them even when the other server was working, and they dubbed her their first friend in Piggott. Actually, Aunt Millie was also becoming their friend.

On the fourth day Jerry was ready to add his first real walk and they walked slowly to the corner and back. Back in the room Brad massaged Jerry's back and his right leg above the cast, using a soothing ointment, having flash studied therapeutic massage while Jerry was in the hospital.

As Jerry lay down to take a nap, Brad set out to visit the Hemingway-Pfeiffer Museum. He walked slowly and checked out everything on both sides of the road. Stopping at a church he read the names on a patch paved with red bricks. Each brick bore the name of someone who had donated money to pay for paving the parking lot which was behind the church. After looking at the parking lot, Brad crossed the alley and met a man working on his lawn. He had been watching Brad reading the names on the bricks and now began a conversation with him. He walked away from his lawn mower and began by introducing himself as the minister of the church. Brad began by telling him he was in Piggott for the first time and was now looking for the Hemingway sights. The minister said, "Hemingway was a free loader when he lived here. He took tons of money from the Pfeiffers and mostly was drunk. They even had a movie premier here for his story *A Farewell to Arms*. Hemingway was too drunk to make it to the premier and then complained bitterly about missing it. So, Uncle Gus offered to send him and Pauline on a Safari to Africa to placate him."

Brad chose to defend Hemingway and said, "Actually, Hemingway paid Gus back by giving him the original manuscripts of two of his novels. Today those manuscripts would sell for at least a million dollars each and Gus only gave them $25,000 for their safari."

The minister continued his criticism, "Well Hemingway just isn't all that well liked here. The Pfeiffers gave him everything and he walked out on Pauline to have an affair with that blonde reporter."

"Martha Gellhorn," Brad responded, "and he married her, so it was much more than just an affair."

'Well anyway, enjoy your visit to the Pfeiffer house and barn. You might want to go down this alley here and go to the library first. They have some items in there relating to Hemingway."

"Thank you for telling me that. I'll go there now. I have looked forward to visiting here for several years and am very excited to be here. By the way, you can thank Hemingway for putting Piggott on the map. And the Pfeiffer mansion is now known as the Hemingway-Pfeiffer Museum."

Brad walked away quickly so no further discussion could take place. He walked down the alley the minister had pointed to and went to see what was on display in the library. When he entered the library there was only one woman there and she was talking to the librarian. There didn't seem to be anything on Hemingway in the display cases, but there was a selection of Dos Passos first editions. Brad assumed they had belonged to Hemingway or else to the Pfeiffer family. He did notice a complete section on Genealogy. When he left the library, he decided to sit under a tree and just look at Piggott from his relaxed position.

After sitting about ten minutes he got up and walked slowly uphill to the museum, noticing the houses as he passed. One of them was in the process of installing an aluminum roof. All of them appeared quite small compared to Oak Park houses. Suddenly a small black dog ran across the street and began to walk along with him. They walked together, the dog usually a few feet above Brad on the hillside, until they arrived at the education center, which was just outside the Hemingway-Pfeiffer House Museum. Brad decided to go into the education center. The dog decided to turn around and head back downhill. As he entered the education center, Brad was greeted by a woman with whom he had had a phone conversation while planning this trip. She seemed very happy that he was there, and they talked for about a half hour. They each had a long history of visiting various Hemingway sites, listening to lectures on Hemingway, and attending Hemingway Conferences. She had not yet been north to Oak Park or to Walloon Lake and Petoskey but told Brad she hoped to go to both places soon.

After the conversation which made him feel very welcome at the museum, he went to the bookstore to sign up for a tour of the house and barn. There were only two others there for the tour, a couple in their thirties. She seemed excited and ready to go, but he appeared to be there only because he was with her. The three of them walked along behind the tour guide, a woman about 70 something Brad guessed, and listened to her recite memorized details. Without showing any excitement, she pointed out original Pfeiffer owned furniture and told any related stories she knew. When they entered a large bedroom, she sat in a chair and motioned to them to sit across from her. They then participated in a very relaxed conversation. This was the room where Ernest's son had decided he was dying. Having been raised in Paris, when his temperature was 102 degrees, he thought of the Celsius scale and believed he wouldn't live much longer. That story, *A Day's Wait,* wasn't one that Brad remembered reading although he did read it that night back in their room.

"I think that was his middle son," the tour guide said.

"No, actually it was his first son, Bumby, who was raised in Paris," Brad informed her. She seemed surprised that a visitor knew more than she did about Hemingway.

After the tour Brad bought some post cards and talked to the woman at the cash register. She introduced herself as Sue, a five-year employee of the museum. He explained about his giving tours in Oak Park, and they exchanged stories of Hemingway, his writing, and his wives. He almost wanted to start giving tours there, but realizing how completely Jerry relied on him, he refrained from doing so. From what he had seen so far it appeared all the tour guides in Piggott were retired women. After their conversation he left to go to the B&B and see if Jerry was up.

Jerry was up and reading in the easy chair. He greeted him with, "Another item crossed off your bucket list."

"Correct, and I really enjoyed it. We'll go back soon when you are walking better."

"Fair enough. I like big old Victorian houses."

"But not Hemingway?"

"I've told you fifty times I don't love Hemingway as much as you do. The way he treated his friends and especially the way he treated his wives. And with four intelligent wives, why did he need affairs on the side? I like *A Farewell to Arms* and *Big Two-hearted River,* but most of his other writings I can live without. "

"If you don't love Ernie, why did you attend all of my lectures and most fund raisers at the Oak Park Foundation?"

"That is what a best friend does. Hell, you even came to the opera with me not once but twice and you listen to Merle Haggard and Johnny Cash and Willie "pot head" Nelson. We are good together even if not all our interests are in total sync."

"I agree. Best times are traveling together," Brad said.

"Spot on bro. I really enjoyed our trip to Virginia a couple of years ago. Remember when we camped in West Virginia and went hiking along the road to pick up beer cans which had been tossed out of cars? Most of the ones we found we hadn't seen in Chicago. Are any of those still in the basement?"

"Not anymore. I decided to recycle them so my sister would have more room to do laundry."

"As we were looking for cans, we came to a small waterfall. We decided to name it on the theory no one had done so before. Boss Falls after Chicago's Mayor Papa Daley, Da Boss."

"Then we got political and decided being President was too big a job for one man so we would run on the independent ticket of the Boss Party as coequal Presidents. We would eliminate hunger in the United States, cut way back on military spending, make preschool education universal and free, cut taxes on people earning less than $250,000 a year, eliminate give aways to the rich and powerful to pay for it, and tax incomes over $750,000 at a higher rate to pay for all our promises."

"Yes, and protect far more federal land from development, plant two million trees on federal land, reduce coal energy by 20 percent a year every year until there were no more coal fired plants, make polluting industries pay 105 percent of all clean-up costs, and move toward health care for all in a single payer plan."

"So why haven't we run yet?"

"Money." Jerry said quickly.

"No, actually it was because you decided to invade Canada and make non-French Canadian provinces states 51 through 59," Brad corrected him.

"They would have voted Democratic more than Republican."

"Probably."

"So, let's run in the next election."

"Done. As soon as you raise the first $20,000."

"Dream on old friend."

Brad went into the kitchen to get them each a cup of hot coffee. When he returned, they each sipped coffee slowly with Brad making his frequent slurping sound. When he set his coffee down on the side table he said, "Another great trip was our trip to Europe. Paris, Amsterdam, Copenhagen and London."

"Only downside there was we stayed in the cheapest hotels, so the bus dropped us off last and picked us up first," Jerry said remembering their trip with equal pleasure.

"Oh well, we did get to see a bit more from the bus windows."

"I so loved Paris. Remember on the Champs-Elysées we spotted two beautiful girls and sat down with them?"

"Of course,' Jerry said emphatically. "You picked up Roseann and took her to dinner the next night leaving me alone in Paris. Some friend you were."

Brad said, defensively, "No problem for you. You had a few too many that evening and ended up with a Korean girl."

"Who flew to London to be with me again and offered to fly to Chicago if I wanted her to."

"You should have invited her."

"I wasn't in love like you were," Jerry said.

"Not in love, but at least halfway there. Roseann was an American studying in Paris, and I so wanted her to keep in touch, but she decided not to."

"But you always tell me your goodnight kiss that night was the best of your life."

"True. It was. I told her you sent her your best greetings and she asked if the kiss was from Jerry, too. I said definitely not, that was me saying I like you very much. I gave her my e-mail and even my home phone number for when she came back to the United States. Since that was almost four years ago, I have decided she isn't ever going to call. Maybe in a week or two I'll kiss Lynda and see how that goes."

"Take her out first, and don't drive her away because she has started to massage me too, and that is quite pleasant. You do it correctly, but nothing feels better than a woman's hands on your body."

"I'll do my best Jeru. She will definitely not stop coming to her Aunt Millie's, so you are safe on that. Now I'm going to the kitchen to prepare dinner."

"Just order a pizza. You don't cook any better than you kiss."

"Screw you."

Brad left the room and went to cook the vegetables and noodles he had bought along with a veggie burger for himself and a hamburger for Jerry made from 90 percent lean and grass-fed beef.

After dinner and back in their room the reminiscences resumed.

"We were on a great double date," Jerry remembered,

"And after the theatre we walked over to Daley Plaza. It was not very busy, and you and Alice decided to dance. So, Vera and I decided to sing *Moon River* to accompany your slow dance. Then we traded places and you two sang *It's all in the Game.* I couldn't tell if you were Nat King Cole or Tommy Edwards, but Alice was definitely Dolly Parton."

"Crazy what you chose to remember. So, what ever happened to Vera? I thought you two would stay together forever."

"I guess she thought so too, but when I wouldn't commit to marriage, she went off with someone else and got married rather quickly."

"Do you ever regret losing her?" Brad asked even though he knew the answer.

"No. If I hadn't broken up with her, I couldn't have fallen in love with Barbara. Of course, if Barbara hadn't left me, I wouldn't have been driving north in Wisconsin not knowing why or where I was going to end up."

"Probably in Little Traverse Bay," Brad opined.

"Knock it off. We agreed it was an accident, and you know it was. Besides, Little Traverse Bay is in Michigan, not Wisconsin."

"Yes, I know, but driving when tired, angry, confused, hurt and lonely to the hilt is not a recipe for a fun trip. You certainly didn't know where you were headed at that point."

"So, let's forget that trip and make this a fun trip," Jerry requested.

"Agreed. But nothing will ever be more fun than our trip to the Maroon Bells in Colorado."

"Yea, I had decided to quit the School of Metaphysics, but I couldn't do it without coming out to talk it over with you. We drove in separate cars so you could go back to class on Monday, but then you didn't go back."

"After two days of talking it over, I knew you were quitting, and I decided to also quit. The easiest way was to just miss class and get kicked out of the school for not doing my exercises."

"Remember then we climbed up the mountain for several hours and then lay down in the sun. After sharing memories of the people and times in the school, we just looked at each other and said it was time to move on. I was so glad you also quit and moved back to Oak Park so we could be the two Bimbo boys together again."

"Bimbo Cookie Cat Man and Bimbo Cake Bat Man."

"Stupid names. Where did we get them?"

"You called Alice and said, 'This is Bimbo Cookie Cat Man" and I almost burst a gasket laughing. Bimbo is derogative and you assigned that name to yourself."

"Well, I do love cookies and I loved my cats too," Brad said."

"So, Alice started calling me Bimbo Cake Bat Man. I guess I do love cake and baseball too. Remind me why you broke up with Alice."

"I thought her sleeping with another man was not too cool. She never could understand my loving the metaphysics thing. And driving 480 miles after work on Friday once a month to cut trees and herd cattle at the College of Metaphysics made no sense to her. She called the school a cult."

"And we drove all the way home on Sunday and somehow got up for work the next morning."

"You never missed a single day of work, right?" Jerry asked?

"Yes, actually I did. The first night I spent with Mary we got a bit drunk. I told her if I had one more drink, I wouldn't be able to drive home. She ran into the kitchen and came back with another pitcher of her favorite vodka mix, Sex on the Beach. We had sex that night on the couch, not on the beach."

"Now I remember. You called in sick after ten a.m. and I was beginning to really worry about you. Then you said Mary was also sick. After that phone call we all talked about the two of you and got no work done until after lunch."

"Think about it. Great sex or a day at work. Which would you choose?"

"Let me think that one over for a day or so."

"Funny man. Welcome back Jeru. I love you like I loved Alice but without the sex."

"Not yet anyway."

"Tomorrow we walk three more houses and return home and each day after that we walk three more houses until you can get all the way around the block."

"What time?"

"Thirty minutes after we finish breakfast. If you are still awake."

Jerry returned the put down, "And if you are both awake and sober."

Brad smiled. Jerry was back to being Jerry again.

Reminiscence

Brad and Jerry were back in their room and Lynda was in the kitchen with Millie.

Jerry asked Brad,

"You really like Lynda, don't you?"

Brad replied, "Stronger than like. It feels like I am beginning to love her. Kind of scary."

"So, tell me how many women you have slept with in your young life so far."

"Young? Thanks. None of your business. Having been my best friend you can figure that out for yourself. Take the number you have slept with and double it and add one more. That should be accurate I think."

"Braggart. You aren't that successful. I'd say take my five and add maybe two."

"Okay. Take your seven and double it."

Jerry said, "Enough already. Just so Lynda believes she is the only one. Or at least the most important one."

"I'll settle for second one because she knows I've been in love once before."

"With whom? Passavant Debutant or Mariel Hemingway?"

"No. Alice. You know that as well as I do. Smarty punk."

"Who is the most famous one?"

"No one there at all. I'd say Phyllis in the School of Metaphysics. She slept with the founder of the school and with the area director, so by osmosis I slept with a mildly famous person or two."

"How about your debutante?"

Brad said, "I wish. You know she was the daughter of the richest man involved with the Passant Cotillion which is the most prestigious cotillion in Chicago. I wrote her a wonderful letter. After all, we novelists can write well."

"How is your novel coming?"

"Don't interrupt me like that. I have listed five possible titles and am mulling them over."

"Great start. I'm blown away."

"Okay Dingy Dongy," Brad said. "Back to my story. So, ten days after I mail the letter, I drive up to talk to her. Biggest mansion I have ever been in. Her Dad answers the door. He is friendly but the look of disbelief is obvious. He leaves me in the large marble entryway and goes inside and calls her from just inside the door. Two minutes later she comes through the door. Just as beautiful as her picture. Maybe even more so. I introduce myself as Brad who wrote the amazing letter. She smiles. What letter? She never saw it. Still, she talks to me for more than a half hour. I get her address at Vassar and damn near kissed her but thought better not to yet. Two days later she goes back to college, and I wait a week and write to her. Another A-plus letter. And quickly an A-plus answer from her. But she can't see me on spring break because she is skiing with friends in Vail. If she had invited me to Vail, we would be married now, but my letter after spring break went unanswered. Too much time. Lost momentum. Probably a new boyfriend for her by that time too. So, no. I felt a rapport with her, but end of story."

"And that local girl? Reprise that one for me."

"I saw a picture of an attractive girl who had just graduated from Dominican University. She had won some award and her picture was in the local paper. I decided to try a different approach, so I called her and told her my name was Reginald and I was working on a thesis on goals of local college graduates. I needed a couple more interviews and wanted to take her to dinner to do an in-depth interview. She agreed and I got her address and went to pick her up that Friday. Her mother checked me out as I waited for her in the living room. I kept silently repeating my name is Reginald and I am in graduate school researching goals for my thesis. I must have passed muster because she smiled and let Julie go to dinner with me. Maybe the bouquet of roses helped persuade her. So, I walk her to my car, the daughter, not the mother, and realize she doesn't have that spark I am looking for. At the restaurant we order dinner and I get a beer and she gets a Pepsi. By now it is clear I am in a dead-end alley."

Brad took a sip of coffee and seemed to be gathering his thoughts.

After a minute or so he said, "I smile and ask her what goals she has for her life. I am looking for people who want to make a major difference in the world, maybe be a scientist or a doctor or a politician with some lofty goal like ending AIDS or ending hunger or cleaning up our oceans. She sort of shrugs and says nothing like any of those things. Maybe get a decent job and get married and have two kids. I'm searching for a good follow-up question and say lots of people your age are committed to some cause and want to find the correct group to work with to make the world a better place. Not really me she says. I just want a safe place to buy a house and raise my children. So rather than waste a good evening I make up three other interviews I had done and tell her one girl wants to save African wildlife, one wants to stop the global warming problem, and one wants to live with uncontacted tribes deep in the Amazon and create a written language for them from their conversations. I embellish with anything I can think of, and she just eats and looks at me as I am talking away. I drive her home, walk her to the door and almost skip to the car. What a bum idea that was. Most boring person I ever bought dinner for."

"So finally, Mariel Hemingway," Jerry asked.
Brad, who loved to talk about himself, took up that story with pride.
"We were both giving tours of the Ernest Hemingway Birth House for several years when Mariel came to Chicago to sell one of her books. You and me giving tours, not Mariel and me. I took the train downtown and got to the bookstore at least an hour early. Killed a bit of time sitting on a bench outside the hotel. Went outside the building and watched people walking by. Went back inside. Then the bookstore man comes to the desk behind half a dozen stacks of her book. I buy the first one he sells. I sit down. Twenty minutes later some radio woman comes in to interview Mariel and following her is Mariel looking as beautiful as her pictures. Somewhat interesting interview. Seems her father Jack drank too much. I loved Jack and didn't want to hear that. He spoke at Ernie's 100th birthday dinner in Oak Park, and I loved him. Then I read *Misadventures of a Fly Fisherman*

44

and enjoyed that too. Anyway, when she had finished the interview Mariel sat down to autograph her books. I did not push and was about fifteenth in line. When it was my turn, I handed the book to the bookstore chick to hand to Mariel to sign to hand to the other bookstore chick to hand back to me. I pointed out I had a 3 by 5 card with the book and Mariel was invited to take my tour of her grandfather's birth house. On the card was my name, my email, my home phone number, and the words Hemingway Birth House Tour. Mariel heard what I said, placed my book in front of her and wrote 'To Brad, I'm Coming. Mariel Hemingway.' She kept the card and I felt on top of the world. I waited for the phone call or the email, but she never called, never emailed, never came. So after about three weeks I sent her a long letter. We novelists write great letters. I addressed it to her via her publisher, which is the proper way to do it. In my letter I said maybe you think I will ask you for money. I promise you I will not. I will pick you up anywhere, hotel, train station, airport. I will take you to dinner with a glass of wine. Can't be too careful here as her dad and granddad drank a bit too much."

"A bit?'

"Well more than a bit, definitely too much. Continuing my letter, you might think I will want to have sex with you. Not the reason for the invite. You can bring your boyfriend or your daughter or both. No charge to them either. Maybe you don't want other people on the tour. I asked our chairman, and he gave me permission to do anything I wanted to do. We can tour at 8 a.m., 7 p.m., midnight, anytime you choose. I have a key to the house and know where all the light switches are. Then I put a small envelope addressed to me inside with her letter and both envelopes had two Hemingway stamps on them. I was giving the post office a few cents at fifty cents postage but felt that was the best way to go. I never got anything back. Inside my envelope was a small card with three boxes to mark; I'm coming turn card over for info on where and when, I don't want to come, and finally, stick it you know where, you knucklehead."

"You didn't."

"No, of course not. I rewrote it with just the first two choices. I do have a modicum of common sense. I await her reply now, three plus years later."

"So bottom line; no sex with debutants, no sex with recent college grads, and no sex with Hemingway granddaughters."

"I put it this way, no sitting at a table sharing a glass of wine and conversation with the most wonderful debutant ever, none with boring recent college grads, and also none with any of Hemingway's granddaughters."

"And no contact from the beautiful Roseann from Paris after the best kiss of your life."

"Don't keep rubbing it in. You lost Barbara and one or two others you hoped to keep."

"Here comes Lynda. That was a great salad we had today, wasn't it?"

"Absolutely. Hi Honey. Come here to your sweetie."

Lynda made a face of disapproval as she came over and sat next to Brad on the bed. He hoped she had not overheard any of his stories.

Brad gets to know Piggott

Six weeks after the boys arrived in Piggott and while having their usual lunch at the café Lynda informed them that the dishwasher had quit. Brad had said when Jerry was better, he would like to work somewhere to earn a little spending money. The café owners told her she could offer him the job. He wouldn't earn very much, but he didn't need much. They worked it out so that he and Jerry would come for lunch each day and then he would start work at 1:30 and work until finished about 5:30. He would earn $30 a day and be paid each Saturday. If the tips for any day exceeded $60 total for the two servers, he would get 20 percent of the excess amount. Brad was no longer calling Jerry's mother as Jerry was now responsible for his own calls, so he and Lynda would leave work when all the pans were clean and put away. They would walk home different ways, stop at the store for groceries, mail something at the post office, or just sit on a bench and talk. Dinner at home then began after 7 p.m., more like in Europe than in a typical Piggott household.

Mondays Lynda got together with her two best friends, both named Laurie. You could tell them apart in writing as one of them spelled her name Lorey. Usually, they had lunch and went for a walk around the main square. Laurie asked Lynda what the two young men from Oak Park were like. All the details don't hold anything back.

"Well," Lynda said "Brad has shown an interest in me. He looks at me with a look I can only describe as a mix of admiration and desire. He is very intelligent and knows almost everything there is to know about Ernest Hemingway. He sings a lot, mostly country songs by Johnny Cash or Hank Williams. Not the best voice I've ever heard but he doesn't sing for anyone else but himself."

"What does he look like? Handsome?"

"Not bad. I'd say he is about five foot eleven. Long hair for a man which is not true blonde, maybe best described as dishwater blond. Sort of subtle tan to brown tones mostly near the ends, and a cute curling which is both subtle and natural. His eyes are blue but not blue alone but with flecks of darker spots maybe like the brown tips of his hair. No, more like emerald and olive drops in a sea of blue. It is hard to tell when he is wearing his glasses. He is near sighted and wears glasses all the time except to bed or to look closely at something printed. He reads quite a bit, mostly literature like Hemingway, Scott Fitzgerald, Steinbeck, and short stories by nearly everyone. He plans to write a novel someday but so far he has only written several short stories and a few poems which he plans to share with me soon."

"What about his friend Johnny?" Laurie asked.

"It's Jerry. He is more handsome but was in a serious automobile accident about two months ago. That left him with a badly broken leg and scratches and now scars on both of his legs, stomach, and chest. He has dark hair, about the same color as mine. I call it off black. His eyes seem turned inward and less interested in me, books, or any surroundings. Like my eyes they are a shade of dark hazel. I liken his moods to PTSD and have started to help Brad massage his legs and work the knees and hips so he will hopefully not limp forever. He is smart, too. They went to school together, not only grade school and high school but also college. A small college somewhere in Iowa. Jerry had a slightly higher grade average and likes to rub it in every chance he gets. Brad majored in English, but Jerry majored in theater and creative arts like painting and sculpture, and he minored in cinema. He hopes to someday produce documentary movies."

"So, which one do you like?"

"Brad has been dating me and we have kissed, and it seems we are falling in love, more so him than me but I am growing more and more interested in him. He might turn out to be the one for me. I am now staying at Aunt Millie's five nights a week because they are only here for six months, barely more than four remaining, and if this is as serious as he seems to want it to be, I need to know what I want before he leaves."

"How wonderful. We must meet them soon."

"I'll try to get us together next weekend. They want to meet you too."

Lynda told Brad it was necessary to meet her two closest girlfriends so the next Sunday they all met for dinner, Brad and Jerry, Lynda, Laurie and Lorey. When all five were seated Lynda said,

"This is my friend Laurie with an a-u."

"Hello Laurie with an a-u, so nice to meet you."

"And this is my friend Lorey with an o."

"Hello Lorey with an o, so nice to meet you, too."

"Nice to meet you, Brad. And you too, Jerry. Lynda has told us so much about you two. She says you are staying at the B&B for six months, that you are working at the café washing pots and pans, and that you are a Hemingway fanatic."

"Correct on all three counts."

"We are more fond of the Pfeiffers here than we are of Hemingway, but we did study one of his stories in grade school."

"Which one?"

"*Wait One Day*. It is the story of his son raised in Paris who thinks he is dying because he has a temperature of 102 degrees. His middle son I think."

"No, it was Jack, also known as Bumby, his first son by Hadley, who was raised in Paris."

"Oh, right. Anyhow he was sick here in the Paul and Mary Pfeiffer house and he thought 102 degrees was fatal because he was thinking Celsius."

"I didn't remember reading that story until I got here and heard it mentioned on the Hemingway-Pfeiffer Museum house tour. It clearly isn't one of the stories talked about at the society conferences."

"Which conferences?"

"I've been to two of The Michigan Hemingway Society conferences in Petoskey," Brad said.

"I suggest you give a paper on that story at your next conference," Laurie said.

"I will take it under consideration."

The server arrived then, and they all ordered pizza although only Brad ordered his without any meat. All the other four wanted sausage and or bacon on theirs. Brad was also the only one to say he wished he could order a stein of beer with his pizza.

"So how are you doing, Jerry?" Laurie asked. "Lynda told us you tried to knock over a giant tree with your car."

"Something like that." Jerry said. "I am quite a bit better now, but still am doing therapy on my right leg with the help of Lynda and Brad. I can walk on it with only a very small amount of pain, and I replaced my crutches with a cane, so it seems all is going according to schedule."

"Which is?"

"To be healed well enough in six months to return to work in October."

"And how is your novel coming Brad?" Laurie asked.

"I have been so busy helping at the B&B, washing pots and pans, helping Jerry exercise, and wooing Lynda that my novel remains mostly in my head. I do run conversations in my head so they will flow better when I sit down to begin writing."

"Why put off until tomorrow what you can put off until next week?"

"Time flows always forward. I will create writing time very soon."

"I'll believe it when I see something on paper." Lynda said.

"Your Hemingway was a real SOB," Lorey said. "I hate him for the way he treated women. He spit on them, cheated on them, and then left each of them for a younger woman."

"Pretty much true, but that is a small part of his life. He truly loved every one of his four wives.

He was generous almost to a fault. With the exception of Martha, he continued to care about his ex-wives and almost treated them as his harem. And don't forget he had depression the vast majority of his adult life. Nearly everything you said can be traced to his depression."

"He drank far too much. And he threw away his friends like they were banana peels."

"He loved his alcohol, but he wrote every morning, so his drinking did not keep him from his writing. I believe the drinking was the way he treated his depression."

"Write drunk, edit sober."

"Cute expression. Not true of Ernie. He never drank while writing. I'm thinking he never even said that, but if he did, it was said tongue in cheek. It makes for fine sales of T-shirts and magnets anyhow."

"He threw his best friends under the bus, like Gertrude Stein and F. Scott Fitzgerald! He even threw away his sister Marcelline."

"Gertrude Stein sniped at him in writing first; he chose to respond in kind. He never totally loved her but used her to learn about art and to be an early critic of his writing. He wasn't too comfortable with her sex life and one time he walked into her apartment, he had an open invitation to drop in anytime, and he overheard her and Alice B. Toklas expressing themselves during sex and from that point on he was far less comfortable with her. But as you know, while he was enjoying her hospitality, especially her drinks and her art collection, he asked her and Alice to be Bumby's godmothers."

"She taught him to use rhythm and repetition like *A Rose is a Rose is a Rose*."

"Perhaps, but his mother taught him music and much of his rhythmic writing could just as easily have come from music. It angered him that Stein wanted credit for creating Hemingway the writer. He created Hemingway the writer through very hard work and intense ambition."

Lorey came back at Brad, "Fitzgerald saved *The Sun Also Rises* from being a disaster."

"It is true he made some very important suggestions, but he also praised the quality and originality of the text. He told Ernie to reduce the pre-action opening biographies and Ernie looked at them with a critical eye and totally removed them. Almost more important he got Ernie to move over to Charles Scribner's Sons where Maxwell Perkins became his editor. The gift that keeps on giving."

"Are you going to defend him against everything I believe?"

"Probably. He was a very complex man. Brilliant, almost total recall, creative, hardworking, original, always teaching someone, generous. Also troubled, ambitious, bold appetites, accident prone, frequently falling in love, shy and insecure. Bottom line there is no one else like him and everyone knows him and most either love him or hate him."

Lorey replied quickly, "You love him, and I hate him. When he lived here, he was a freeloader living on the wealth of his in-laws. Uncle Gus gave Pauline and him a house, a car, a safari in Africa, company stock, more than one car actually, and plenty more."

"Yes, he did. He very much liked Ernie," Brad said.

"Ernie responded by giving Gus two original manuscripts worth millions of dollars today."

"And Ernie asked for them back."

"Only after Uncle Gus withdrew all support and said the stock belonged to his two sons by Pauline and not to Ernie."

"Time out." Laurie with an a-u interjected. "Enough yin and yang of Hemingstein. Lynda wanted us to get to know you, not find out how much you know about a writer. So tell us Brad, what is your last name?"

"Hull"

"How can you give up six months of a decent salary to live on dividends and washing pots?"

"I had no choice. Jerry and I are best friends, but it is more than that. We are almost like identical twins. We met in third grade and have been together almost every day since then. It all started with a little girl in our third-grade class. We sat on opposite sides of her and two rows behind. She had blond curls and freckles and thought she was god's gift to third grade boys. We hatched a plot to throw wads of paper at her at the same time. We did that three times and then Miss Codanti called us up to her desk. She told us we were kicked out of her class and would only be let back in when we came to school with our mothers. We left and walking home we agreed not to tell our mothers, but to meet in the park and get an extra day or two off school. During dinner that night Jerry's mother called my mother and we four went to school together at 9 o'clock the next morning. At first, I was angry that Jerry had told his mother, but while our mothers talked to Miss Codanti who stood holding the classroom door open, we ran and played in the hall and the rest of the class talked and played inside the classroom. It seemed to last forever and certainly the conversation lasted more than a half hour. After that we walked to school together and to this day, we still do nearly everything together.

"In high school Jerry was at my house playing cards nearly every day. He finishes my sentences, we read many of the same books, we love the same TV shows, we sing many of the same songs, we laugh at the same jokes, we often wear identical shirts, I call his mother 'mom' and he calls my mother 'mother number 2.' So, when one evening in April Jerry went on a camping trip to Wisconsin and he didn't tell me where he was going and he didn't ask me to come along, I had this terrible foreboding. He had been depressed for about three weeks and I knew he wouldn't get over it for at least another several weeks."

Brad paused for a sip of sweet tea and chose how to tell about Jerry's accident.
"I went to bed early that night but didn't fall asleep, and about 11 o'clock I sat upright and held my head in my hands. I just kept saying 'no, damn it no, no, no,' but I wasn't sure exactly why. A few hours later the phone rang, and mom - his mom - told me he was in the hospital in some town in Wisconsin after being in a serious car accident. I told her to sit still and drink a cup of tea and I'd pick her up about 5 a.m. and we'd drive up to see him and be there when the hospital opened for visitors in the morning.

"She wanted him to move back with her when he got out of the hospital, but he told me after nine years of living on his own, actually nine years living with me, he couldn't put up with his mother twenty-four hours a day. After our first three visits to the hospital, I decided the best course was to take him somewhere far from Oak Park to recover at his own pace and away from everyone who knew him. Since I had been wanting to see Piggott and the famous Pfeiffer barn, I told him we would come down here for six months. Money can't compete with friendship, but I get my best dividends in March, so I had money in my savings account. I called down here and Aunt Millie was very helpful in agreeing we could live here for six months at a reduced rate. She took her weekly rate and reduced it somewhat and said I could get another little bit off that by washing dishes, helping in the garden, vacuuming, and various other chores like doing our own laundry. I sold a few shares of my best stock to jack up the checking account and we are fine so far, but I would have sold anything I owned if that was necessary to help Jerry."

"Even your autographed *The Old Man and the Sea*?"

"Of course, even that. Lynda has certainly filled you in on me for you to know what I have in my safety deposit box in my bank back home."

"I pry. I seek. I find. She also told me you like to talk, and you might have just won the blue ribbon for the longest answer to a simple question this year. Next question, shorter answer please. How much do you love her?"

"The heart has unlimited amounts of love, yet I believe that unlimited amount only begins to tell my love for her."

56

"Deeper than the deepest ocean, higher than the sky?" said Laurie.

"Yes."

"A one-word answer. Impressive. So, if she moves to Oak Park as Mrs. Hull where does Jerry live?"

"I say with us, but the three of us will have to have serious discussions on that and arrive at a course that is best for all three of us. He won't come on our honeymoon, but if he doesn't live with us, at a minimum we will have dinner together three or four times a week. Minimum."

Laurie continued her questions, "Must Lynda work as a server in Oak Park?"

"No. Another serious discussion. She will have the final say on where or even if she works. I wouldn't mind if she stayed at home and played with her cat."

"Have you ever done anything selfish or mean?"

"I'm human. Of course I have, but not very often."

"Name one thing."

"In college our roommate was taunting me, and I felt rather than argue I'd express my displeasure by knocking his pile of books on the floor. I swept my arm up to the books and slowly pushed them off the dresser and onto the floor. As they hit the floor, I realized that was a terrible thing to do. Don loved his books."

"Another thing."

"Okay," Brad said slowly while choosing how to answer.

"I give tours at the Hemingway Birth House in Oak Park. Occasionally a visitor will leave something behind. Usually, they realize what they did and return to claim it. Many visitors go to the Frank Lloyd Wright Home and Studio before coming to Hemingway. They sell a nice address book at Frank's house with pictures of his architecture between address pages. About three years ago such a book was left behind by a visitor. I would guess the cost at $29. Probably a bit more. We carefully noted it was left by a visitor and waited for him or her to come back and claim it. After two months or so it was put into the dresser drawer out of sight. I noticed it at least ten times while volunteering after that and decided the visitor was never coming back for it. No one else did anything about it, so after six months of waiting I decided to take it home and use it for my address book. Since the owner would never be back it seemed a waste to let it sit in the dresser forever. Sort of finders keepers when the owner is untraceable. And I made a small donation to the foundation in our change jar."

'Anything recently?"

"Ask Jerry."

"Jerry?"

Jerry thought a minute and then said, "Brad has gone to the Hemingway-Pfeiffer Museum six or seven times leaving me home alone. That is a little bit selfish. Of course, each time he did ask me if I wanted to come with him, so the emphasis is on the word a little bit."

"That's three words."

"True," Jerry agreed with her.

After another short pause he added, "Actually I am not too comfortable with you grilling my friend. He is as good a person as there is anywhere in Illinois or now in Arkansas."

"Dessert anyone?" Lynda asked.

No one said yes so, they waved for the check. Brad paid it and Lorey and Laurie left a generous enough tip.

On the way home Brad said, "I like your girlfriends. We'll do other things with them again soon."

"I didn't tell Lorey to quiz you like that," Lynda said apologetically. "I was a bit embarrassed, but I liked all your answers, even the longest answer to a simple question this year."

"So, I like to talk," Brad said.

"Good pizza," Jerry said.

The Outing

Right on time Laurie arrived at the B&B. Breakfast was served at 8 a.m. every day and minutes before eight she joined the other three at the breakfast table, three because Lynda was now there at every breakfast having stayed the night. Millie often served breakfast to neighbors and friends for a small fee which helped her meet expenses, but she wouldn't hear of Laurie paying. This morning they had waffles, omelettes, fruit, juice, and coffee. The coffee pot was always kept full whenever guests were staying there. After everything was served Millie sat down with them because they were family to her and no longer only paying guests. They all felt it was a perfect day to be walking in the woods, not hot and not cold, not raining and just a soft cooling breeze. This was one of those special days when things all turned out exactly as one wished.

Two weeks after the pizza evening Brad, Jerry, Lynda, Lorey and Laurie planned a day of hiking with a picnic lunch. Even though Jerry still walked with a cane he felt he was up to a hike of two miles or less. They selected the Ozark National Scenic Riverways where the girls had been hiking twice before. The evening before their outing Lorey called Lynda to say something had come up and she could not make it. The other four decided they would go as planned. Brad and Lynda spent over an hour in the kitchen making sandwiches, washing fruit and baking cookies. The food would go into backpacks and each of the other three would carry something for Jerry. He said he could manage a backpack, but Lynda would not allow it. They divided everything they would take with them into three backpacks.

Laurie hugged Millie goodbye as she was like a mother to her. They got into Brad's car with Jerry and Laurie in the back seat and Lynda in the front passenger seat serving as navigator. Driving north they decided to sing songs they all knew. First was *John Jacob Jingle Hymerschmidt.* Then *Plant a watermelon seed upon my grave.* Lynda and Laurie sang *Kumbaya,* and Brad and Jerry joined after the first line of each verse. Brad added a verse 'Someone is screaming Lord, Kumbaya.' Jerry put in 'Someone is kissing Lord, Kumbaya.' The girls decided to move on to *The Battle Hymn of the Republic* and *America the Beautiful.* Then Brad suggested *Burning Ring of Fire,* but the girls only knew the chorus which they also sang. Jerry suggested *On the Road Again* and after that they went to conversation and no more singing.

"Tell me more about your trip to Europe," Laurie said.
"One fun thing," Jerry said. "We went to Versailles as a side trip from Paris. Brad and I agreed should one of us win the Lottery we would build or buy a Chalet in the French countryside not far from Paris. No luck yet on that, but it seems like the Chalet will be in his novel coming in about ten years."
"Cute." said Brad.
"I mentioned Versailles," Jerry continued, "because we had each bought peaches to take with us and we sat under the magnificent Linden trees and ate our peaches. Then as a gift

to the people of France we dug a hole and planted peach trees in line with the Lindens. Next time any of us is in Paris check and see how the peach trees are doing."

"That is the highlight?"

"One of them, yes. Versailles is a lovely weekend home. For a King. Another highlight is dining. Breakfast of fresh pastries and breads and cold cuts and cheese and fruit. We always managed to stash a bit to eat later. Dinners in wonderful restaurants. Our favorite was Le Procope in Paris. We took a cab with three others on the tour. It is the oldest restaurant continuously serving in all of Paris. I could hardly believe it opened in 1686. We wanted to see the Ben Franklin room and our waiter took us upstairs to see it. Franklin was our ambassador to France for a time and he had a private dining room on the upper level overlooking the street. We all wanted to go back 220 years or so and dine with Ben, but his only presence today is a bust of old Ben and a few items from his time. On a landing at a turn in the staircase we spotted a hat behind glass which had belonged to Napoleon. We found out it is a big tourist attraction. The story goes rather than pay for dinner he left his hat as collateral and never reclaimed it. It is things like that that make me love Paris. And the food, *tres bien*."

"Do you speak French?"

"*En plus mon cherie*."

Brad joined in, "We have tapes of French and we sit and drink wine from France and listen to the tapes. When we get back to Paris, we will talk French and learn more in two weeks than we learned from the tapes. About all we can say now is how are you, I am fine, thank you, and we can count to ten, or eleven on a good day. And *Bon Sang* and *Merde*."

"Which mean?"

"Damn it and shit."

"You could have left that out," Lynda said.

"Tell us your highlights," Laurie said.

Brad continued, "Besides Paris, Eiffel Tower, Sacré Cœur, Notre Dame, and Hemingway's Café de Flore and Brasserie Lipp, I'd say Tivoli Gardens in Copenhagen. It would be better with you two with us, but we loved the rides and the ambience and of course the food. We went with three others from the tour again and Jerry always sat with the lady and left me with the panting old dude from Idaho. Nice guy though, we got email addresses from most of our travel companions. One or two exchanges and now nothing for over two years."

Brad decided to ask each of them to name his or her favorite novel. "I'll go first. Think a minute about it. As a Hemingway docent I will choose one of Ernie's though I love them all, I pick *A Farewell to Arms*. Who goes next?"

"I can," Jerry said. "*This Side of Paradise* by F. Scott Fitzgerald."

Laurie spoke up next, "*To Kill A Mockingbird* by Harper Lee. We still haven't learned how to treat people of color with fairness and equality. Lynda's turn."

"Okay, I'll pick *Pride and Prejudice* by Jane Austen. I've read it three times and have seen two different movies made from the novel, and I still love it."

Brad said, "Last one to answer picks the next question."

Lynda thought a moment and chose, "you said you wrote a poem or two. Let's each pick a favorite poem. I love so many, but mine will be *Do Not Go Gentle into That Good Night* by Dylan Thomas. *Rage, rage against the dying of the light.*"

Laurie went second, "Easy for me, *The Road Not Taken* by Robert Frost. When your Hemingway couldn't speak at the inauguration of John F. Kennedy, Kennedy chose Robert Frost as his speaker. Just about the best poet ever, at least in English. *Two roads diverged in a yellow wood.* Jerry?"

Jerry chose quickly "*If* by Rudyard Kipling. *If you can keep your head when all those about you are losing theirs and blaming it on you, you'll be a man my son.* Next, Brad is last because he is least."

Brad said, "I love you too. I pick *Fair Daffodils* by Robert Herrick. I memorized it at Grinnell and every spring when the Daffodils bloom in our yard I recite it to them morning and evening. *Fair Daffodils I weep to see thee haste away so soon.* Time out, can we have a runner up for this category? We need to include Shakespeare. For runner up I pick his sonnet *Let me not to the marriage of true minds.* Okay?"

"Excellent choice," said Jerry, and both girls were fine with that choice. Brad thought they probably would take some time to remember any other Shakespeare sonnet anyway.

"Read us your sonnet." said Laurie. "Lynda said you wrote one."

"When we get home, I'll get it out and read it. I wrote it four years ago and when I recite it, I mess up a few words here and there."

"Next category will be favorite song. I choose *Sunday Morning Coming Down* by Kris Kristofferson as sung by Johnny Cash."

"Two out of three of us have heard you sing that already," said Lynda. Brad sang that song nearly every day and she and Jerry had heard it many times.

Lynda continued, "I choose *His Eye is on the Sparrow*, my favorite hymn, or at least tied for favorite. *His eye is on the Sparrow, and I know he watches me.* Tied is *I come to the Garden Alone.*"

Laurie went next, "Has to be the Beatles. I pick *Eleanor Rigby*, although *I want to Hold Your Hand* is just about tied. Your turn Jerry."

Jerry picked, "*Imagine* by John Lennon. *Imagine all the people living life in peace.*"

He then sang the rest of the verse and did a respectable imitation of Lennon.

"You pick now Jerry," said Laurie.

"No, let Brad pick again. He loves this exercise."

"Actually, not totally true," said Brad.

"But I choose name your favorite city anywhere in the world. Mine is Paris, of course, both because of Hemingway and because of the great time Jerry and I had there."

"And the one who got away," said Lynda. "I choose San Francisco."

Jerry chose, "Chicago. Called the second city but clearly as great as Boston, New York, Denver, New Orleans, and San Francisco. Laurie?"

"Guess I better choose a foreign one since you named so many of the main American ones. So many great ones, uhm, uhm, okay. I choose Prague."

"Great choice." said Brad. You can now pick the category, but first I pick München as runner up city."

"Fine by me," said Laurie. "Category is person, living or dead, you would choose to dine with tonight. I would love to meet and talk to Barbra Streisand. Wonderful singer and fighter for gay and women's rights. She can hold a high note longer than anyone else alive."

"Brad spoke up quickly, "So as not to be last, I choose Ernest Miller Hemingway. But you all knew that."

"Jerry spoke next, "He not only wants to meet him, he wants to talk to him in his dreams and once did. I would like to dine with Johann Wolfgang von Goethe. Possibly the smartest person who ever lived according to Einstein who is no slouch himself. Lynda?"

Lynda said, "I choose Nelson Mandela. To come out of so long a time in jail and forgive and love and lead South Africa out of apartheid. Truly a great man."

She then added, "We're almost there now. Follow my directions carefully Brad. There is a road angling off to the right in just a short distance and we want to take it."

When the car was parked at the trail head, they all got out, three put on their backpacks, and they discussed which trail to follow. It had to be the easier one because of Jerry's slight mobility problem which he said didn't matter, but again Lynda would have none of it. A quick snack of an apple for everyone except Jerry who ate a peach and planned to plant the pit as a gift to the people of Missouri.

They walked and talked. They looked at interesting trees. The tried to name the birds they spotted. At a clearing they sat down to eat lunch. Jerry then informed them he would wait here and join them on the walk back. He didn't think it wise to run out of energy at the far end of the trail. Lynda did not want to make him wait alone for what could be two hours so she said she would wait with him, and Brad and Laurie should continue a while and then come back and join them. Brad hesitated but then agreed it was best not to leave Jerry alone and he and Laurie would enjoy walking a few more miles.

After they were out of earshot of the others Laurie said, "It was terrible the way Lorey attacked you at the pizza night. I like Hemingway far more than she does and can see why you enjoy him so much. I reread *The Old Man and the Sea* last year and got so much more out of it the second time."
"That is usually the case. Hemingway is layered and most of us miss a good part of what can be inferred or implied. Don't worry about Lorey as I can take it and if need be, dish it out."
"Well, you were almost too patient with her. I might have thrown a beer in her face if she talked that way to me."
"Let's not get into throwing wine or beer in people's faces. I plan never to do that to anyone. I'd rather drink it all anyway. Next time I'll just say *Merde* and she probably won't even understand what I said. Speaking of *Merde,* I

have a letter in my safety deposit box Ernie sent to his son Jack in 1959. I had to have it because he addressed it to Bum. Dear Bum. Jack would have been about 36 at the time and his dad still used the baby name Bumby in the letter. He signed it Papa which I also love. In the letter he complained about his eyes bothering him and then wrote *Merde* happens. Having been raised in France the first six years of his life Jack was fluent in French. Jerry almost fell over when he found I spent more than $5,000 just to own that letter."

"How is it that letter was for sale," Laurie asked with surprise in her voice. "Didn't most of his writings end up in the Kennedy Library?"

"Yes. Many others are in university libraries. I figured out Jack's first wife died, and he remarried. His second wife didn't see anything wrong in selling that letter and I must have outbid every other collector."

"Well unlike Lorey with an O I would love to see it someday."

"Visit Lynda and me in Oak Park and I will show it to you."

"I do need to talk to you about Lynda," Laurie said turning suddenly very serious.

"She is my dearest friend. She told me you are planning to propose to her. Is that true?"

"True."

"So do you love her more than any other woman you have ever dated?"

"Yes, very much so. Absolutely."

"Have you ever slapped or punched any woman?"

"No. I am non-violent. I would never hit anyone."

"If she says no to sex some night, what would you do?"

"I guess I would kiss her good night and roll over and try to sleep. If it happened two or three nights in a row, I think I would ask her what her reason was and maybe we could solve some problem together."

"What if she spent more on a new outfit than you had budgeted?"

"I don't have a budget for individual items like clothes or transportation. I just try to spend about 95 to 98 percent of my income each month. If we spent over our monthly income some time, I'd transfer some funds out of savings. Big items might require the sale of some stock to build up savings."

"Would you help her in the kitchen and with the house cleaning? Would you change the baby's diapers at 2 a.m.?

"Yes, on all three. I would like us to cook together, garden together, take turns on the diapers and the bottles and the feeding and walking the floor with a crying child."

"I ask you these things because I know she will want to discuss her answer with me when you propose. We were the two best sprinters in women's track, and she always beat me in the quarter mile by a half second. We share everything. We joined Girl Scouts together, vacationed together twice, to Daytona Beach, Florida and to the Grand Canyon. She is the sweetest, kindest, most fun person I know, and I am so happy to see you two in love. You are the first man she dated who I think is good enough for her. Take care of her and love her as much as I do. Promise?"

"I promise."

After an awkward pause Brad said, "Interesting sidebar. Jerry and I ran track in high school, and he almost always beat me by a quarter second in the quarter mile. So even if I beat every runner on the other team, I still didn't win the race."

Laurie said, "Lynda did say you were a bit irreverent and had had quite a few girlfriends. Are you sure you are ready for this commitment?"

"Absolutely. I thought I was in love a few times, but now I know I am. There is a whole new level of love I feel for her. You see this on Hallmark movies, but it was never so absolute for me before Lynda, and what is better it is more real every day we spend together."

"That is what I needed to hear."

They walked without talking for a few minutes.

To break the awkward silence Laurie asked, "Do you and Jerry go for bike rides often? Lynda and I go for ten or fifteen-mile bike rides at least every other week."

"No, we don't, but we did take a 240-mile bike ride two years ago. There is an old railroad bed between Elroy and Sparta, Wisconsin which was made into a bicycle trail. We decided to ride that trail and then continue biking until we got home. Jerry's younger brother Philip had just graduated from high school and wanted to come with us. Actually, that is probably the only interesting trip I ever took that I haven't told Lynda about."

"Tell me all about it then."

Brad thought about where to start and then said, "A friend drove the three of us up to La Crosse, Wisconsin. Planning to camp on the way home, we had a tent which we set up on an island in the middle of the Mississippi River. We figured to tour the brewery in the morning and then drive to Sparta to begin our trip. Our friend would then drive home to go to work on Monday. In town for dinner three different people told us not to camp in the middle of the river because mosquitoes on that island are large and vicious, but our tent was already up and it was already dark, so we decided to stay there rather than move the tent and try to find somewhere to pitch it after dark. What a night. Nothing we tried kept the mosquitoes off and we each had more than a dozen bites that night. The brewery opened for tours at ten a.m., so we had a leisurely breakfast and arrived for the first tour. Not wanting to ride drunk Jerry and Phil each had one glass of beer, but don't tell Lynda this. I went back three or four times. It isn't every day you get fresh beer for free."

"How much did your girlfriend drink?"

"I didn't say my girlfriend was the driver, did I?"

"No, but" air quote "a friend" air quote "is what you say when you don't want me to know it was your girlfriend driving."

"You are right, it was Alice and she also stopped at one beer."

Brad paused to contemplate how clever Laurie was, then continued, "Alice dropped us off at the start of the bike trail, kissed us all goodbye and left for home. Our intention was to cover an average of 30 miles each day and arrive home Sunday night. Eight days at 30 miles each is the whole 240-mile trip."

Brad paused to take a drink of water and saw Laurie was totally attentive to his story.

He continued, "First part is an old railroad bed, the first in the country I believe to go from rail to trail. It wasn't bad riding, but it wasn't packed hard either and there were often loose stones. It turned out to be a very hot day, so we stopped at the convenient store in the first town and bought a quart of lemonade. We looked at each other when the bottle was empty and agreed at every further stop, we would each buy our own quart. I have never sweated more than on that part of the trip. There are three tunnels on the trail and in the third one Phil did not see a hole which damaged his front wheel. He insisted he needed to do the entire trip with us, so he went into town to get his wheel fixed. About two hours later he was back, but losing that time meant day one we fell quite a bit short of thirty miles. We decided to stop for dinner, set up camp, and push harder the next day. Unfortunately, day two was hotter than day one, so we stopped for drinks and rest like five times and only made twenty-seven miles that day. After Elroy we took the least travelled roads we could find, small two-lane roads and even gravel country roads. Two more days ride we came to Madison where we planned to spend the night at the University. Two pleasant female students said we could sleep in their dorm in the basement lounge area, so we brought our bikes inside and put our sleeping bags on the floor and just then it started to rain outside. The only night so far we slept inside and it rained rather hard. Phil and I were not used to exercise which lasted all day long, so we voted to stay in Madison for a day of rest. We had a pleasant relaxing day getting acquainted with the area near the University. As a compromise with Jerry, we agreed to hit the road earlier than usual."

"Was Jerry anxious to get home?"

"Yes, he still wanted to get to work on Monday. It now looked like we would get home sometime after noon on Monday. The next night we stopped in a small town for the night. The local policeman informed us that camping was not permitted anywhere in the town. He suggested we sleep on the high school roof. Weird as that sounded, he said it was safer than on the ground. We climbed up a fire escape with our gear and slept on the roof. The next night the same thing happened. Local policeman told us no camping permitted. This time his suggestion – or really an order – was for us to sleep in the jail. There was an empty cell, and he left the door open, so the three of us can always say with a straight face that we have spent one night in a jail cell in Wisconsin. Finally, about two p.m. Monday we left Phil at his mother's house where he was staying at that time. Jerry and I crashed at our bungalow about three p.m. We had gone about 20 miles longer than the shortest way to avoid the main highways, and neither of us was quite in shape for the Tour de France."

"That was the most thorough description of a bike trip I have ever heard."

"Oh, one more thing," Brad added. "We came to a very steep hill on a back country road. Jerry and Phil decided to break almost continuously to control their speed, but I decided to just let her rip. At the bottom of the hill my speedometer read a tad over sixty miles an hour. They thought I was crazy, but it was very exhilarating and thankfully I was able to not lose control."

Laurie smiled a mischievous smile and asked Brad, "Can you tell me something about Jerry that Lynda doesn't know?"

Brad thought what to tell her and then answered, "Jerry is my best friend, and I wouldn't say anything negative about him to anyone, but there is one interesting thing I can share. We were both fourteen years old and he had a serious disagreement with his mother about her being too strict and controlling. He told me the next day he felt like running away from home, not for good or anything like that, but maybe for four days or even a week. We were on summer break from school, and I loved the idea. We discussed it and decided to hop a freight train going north to near Minneapolis where it again slowed enough for us to jump off. His dad worked for the Chicago Great Western Railroad until it was purchased by the Chicago and Northwestern Railroad, and he knew where the north bound trains came to a near stop. We decided to buy cans of Sterno and beans and corn and such and bury them near the spot where we planned to hop the train. We did all of that and were going to leave on a Sunday morning while our parents were in church, go dig the supplies up, and hop the freight. I was not at all unhappy with my parents but was excited for the adventure.

"Saturday evening, I had my selected clothes, toothbrush and various supplies in my backpack and was all set to go in the morning and then the phone rang. It was Jerry's mother telling my mother what we had planned. Why he told his mother I'll never know, but of course I had to go alone to dig up the supplies because our parents didn't trust us to go together. I gave them all to him, but happy as I was that he and his mother were no longer at odds, I was quite disappointed that our great adventure never took place. I was excited to be running away from home and I was never at odds enough with my parents to want to do so."

Laurie looked at her watch and said, "Oh my goodness, look at the time. We need to get back. Want to race?"
They ran about 440 yards side by side, started laughing, held hands for about eight seconds, and walked the rest of the way back to the lunch spot in silence. Jerry and Lynda were no longer there, but they caught up with them about halfway back to the car.

Metaphysics

Lynda was curious about Brad's metaphysical beliefs and decided to ask him to explain in detail just what he believed and what he did not believe.

"Why do you say that metaphysics is real, and Jerry says it is mostly a cult of wishful thinkers?" she asked.

Brad thought carefully for thirty seconds or so and then answered her, "Jerry is more into physical things as being real and metaphysics is more of a belief that we create our own reality with our thoughts and our expectations. He tried to create the perfect relationship with Barbara and when she broke up with him, he said it was quite often not possible to create the things in life you truly want."

"He was right then, wasn't he? His entire mind was set on marrying her and he failed to create it, to bring it into reality."

"True enough," Brad said. "But you know the old saying 'when one door closes somewhere another door is opening for you.' You can't create anything with another person unless that person is creating it too, or at least accepting of it."

"So why do you keep saying that what you learned in the school is true? What have you created?"

"My entire life so far. First, I keep a ten most wanted list. I am supposed to read it every single day and put some mental energy into creating those things, number one is most important to me, and number ten is the least important of the ten. My list included getting a six month leave to spend full time with Jerry and I was the first employee in the entire data processing department ever to be granted one. Also, on my list was to have a 401K worth $100,000 by the end of this year. I was on track, before I took the six months leave, to have a few dollars over 100,000 by year end. I also pictured falling in love with a woman who was everything I could wish for which included intelligent, great sense of humor, enjoying travel, happy family situation, not a teetotaler but not a heavy drinker, a good listener, and a good storyteller. Bingo. I met you and you are exactly what I pictured.

"Very important to me and a joke to Jerry is I find a lot of quarters. I put find quarters at number five on my list. Sort of a test of my creative abilities. Soon after that I passed one of those ubiquitous pay stations where you pay to park in Oak Park. On impulse I reached into the coin return and found seven quarters. Seven. Who leaves that much change in the coin return? Maybe luck and not creation using the law of attraction? Next time I reached in I found nothing. I said under my breath 'Come on I deserve at least one quarter.' Eight or ten steps away from the pay station I looked down and there was a quarter on the sidewalk. But what convinced me for real was when Jerry, Phil and I went to a Cubs game. In the sixth inning the skies opened up and it began to pour. After sheltering under a walkway for a while we decided the game wouldn't resume and we would go for a beer. We left Wrigley Field one at a time to run to the nearest bar. Jerry went first and jumped over a puddle. Phil went next and jumped over the same puddle. I brought up the rear and jumped over the puddle but stopped there, reached back, and picked up a quarter from the bottom of the puddle. I hadn't seen it and believe it was my subconscious mind responding to my visualizations of finding quarters. Jerry and Phil don't agree with me, but of course neither of them saw the quarter under two inches of water either. How did I? Successful use of my ten most wanted list and visualization."

"Okay. What about healing, astral projection, past lives?" she said.

"I am not much of a healer, but I have seen more advanced people touch someone and heal them. The thing about healing is that the person being healed must want to be healed. For example, if your father has decided it is time for him to die, you can heal him and the next day he will be just as sick again because his mind is more in control of his body than yours is. My healing successes are small but real. The first healing class I sat in on we were directed to a hospital in Texas where a friend of our teacher was having surgery. I was sitting in the school in Chicago and suddenly I smelled a hospital room, a strong antiseptic smell in the air. I was so shocked I came back into my body immediately, but there was no such smell anywhere near me in the school, so I believe I astral projected to a hospital in Texas for a few seconds.

"The next time was when my cousin had a baby born without any skin covering his stomach. They rushed the baby to the children's hospital across Denver and I was desperate to help him survive. Two days later we had a healing class and I had had a strong picture of the most people there of any class I had ever been to. I walked in with two friends from the

Palatine school. Instead of the usual five there were nine people there to heal my cousin's baby. The director of the Chicago school said she visualized the baby running through the house. When I visited my cousin two and a half years later, little Walter was running through the house. He was the baby with the most severe skin gap ever to survive in the Denver Children's Hospital. And we never had anyone from a different school at our healing classes except that one night."

"So, you didn't heal him but attracted the people who did?" Lynda asked.

"Who can say. Perhaps my strong desire did heal him and the extra people there were just extras. One other healing class I cared about the results was when my Uncle Paul was in the Oak Park Hospital. As a boy he had had his appendix out and dad always called the doctor that did the surgery a bumbling quack. Turns out Uncle Paul was in great pain and his appendix scar was involved. I heard it had twisted and was now blocking something critical. Dad visited his brother Paul in the hospital and said he feared we were going to lose him. He looked terrible and seemed resigned to leave us at the youthful age of 64. At healing class, I submitted Uncle Paul and we all pictured him getting well. Four days later he had recovered and was sent home. I can't say for sure we did it, but two for two is probably not a coincidence.

"Another thing I believe based partly on what I learned in the school is that we have had many past lives. The Christian church doesn't accept reincarnation, but I do along with probably a billion Buddhists, Hindus, and Sikhs. Why? We had past life readings and crossings. We also had regression sessions where we visited ourselves in a past life. Again, I did not see clearly, but in one regression I saw a Norwegian Stave Church. When I paid a reader to do a crossing between my sister and me it came back as a life in Norway. That couldn't be just a coincidence. As a final point, when the director of the school died three of the most advanced teachers went with him to the end of their silver cords and then returned to their bodies as he went on to the afterlife. I can't do what they did but I know them all well and I believe they are telling it as it happened.

"Oh, and on my ten most wanted list was to own a big Mercedes Benz. A couple of years later Jerry went with me to the Dodge dealer to buy a new Dodge. I picked out the one I wanted, and we went outside to consult about it. First used car on the lot was an S500, Mercedes big expensive car. It was seven years old and only had 63,000 miles on the odometer. Price was the same as the new Dodge. Jerry laughed and said to go ahead and buy the Mercedes. I did. I put 75,000 miles on it and then put it up on blocks in my garage where it remains today. Maintenance began to be too much for me to justify. Most comfortable car I was ever in though, and Jerry agrees with that. My area director at my old job drove a black S500 and I always tried to park next to his car to show him a guy making maybe one fourth of what he did drove the same car that he had. So here was an item on my list manifesting like a year after I had stopped picturing it."

"Thank you for that. There is a lot there for me to process."

After another thirty second pause Lynda said, "So how about your writing? Will you share the poems you wrote with me?"
"I will. Other than Jerry and some of my family no one has ever heard these poems. Stay here and I'll go get them."
It took about ten minutes to locate and assemble all his poetry and when he returned Lynda had refilled their coffee cups with hot coffee and brought a sweet roll for each of them. They ate the sweet rolls and began to drink the coffee when Brad began, "I'll start with my take on a Shakespearean Sonnet. Ready?"
"Ready and eager."
Brad read slowly and carefully,

"From birth to death each lonely man must haste
to build upon the shifting sands of time
some monument to stand amid the waste
And loud proclaim 'this life was not in vain'

Some few there are whose gift it is to give
with pen, or paint, cold stone, or acting part
a wondrous work that of itself does live
and thereby make its makers death less hard

Such men are few, the rest are bidden wed,
each with his bride to press on toward his call,
that from the love shared on their marriage bed
springs forth man's greatest work: a newborn soul

Therefore, I mourn the love you kept from me
Without your love I had no need to be."

"Deep and sad. Read another one less sad," Lynda said.
"Okay. This one I titled *I Love You Just Because You Are.*
In the School of Metaphysics we ended each teacher's
weekend at the college with a circle of love. You held hands
with the person on each side of you in the circle. The one on
your right, often someone you didn't know, turned to you,
and said, 'I love you just because you are.' You then turned
to the one on your left and said to that person, 'I love you
just because you are.' It was a moving and powerful
experience. The poem.

You are a seamstress sewing
Alone and late at night
Creating a gown for a grand ball
Bleeding fingers by candlelight
From cloth you're creating beauty
So your child can eat and learn
The path you've chosen is long and hard
I love you just because you are.

You dance each dance belle of the ball
Coyly smiling, tossing your curls,
The men stand in line awaiting the chance
to swirl you across the floor
With laughter and giggles enchanting
Your beauty a legend creating
Your path is paved with gold and myrrh

I love you just because you are.

A child frail and dying
Shivering, choking, crying,
The doctor slowly shakes his head
Your parents linger beside the bed
Unknown the joys of running
Your eyes reflect a knowing
Your path this time does not run far
I love you just because you are.

You walk the halls of power
With diplomatic wisdom
Your speeches recorded and heeded
Determine the course of a nation
Hands raised at the microphone
Thunderous applause for a winner
You've walked the path of a leader
I love you just because you are.

Each one reflects a part of me
The parts become a whole
I too have sewed and danced and died
Have laughed and bled and led and cried
Getting in touch with the parts of me
Learning the way a Christ to be
The varied paths I've walked upon
I love me just because I AM. "

"Better message than the first one," Lynda said. "You have a few more?"

"Yes. A bit more lighthearted, I give you *The Incredible Diving Potato*. I wrote this after a dinner with Jerry and Phyllis, another teacher in the School of Metaphysics. I was so embarrassed that I picked up the entire potato and watched it dive into the gravy, totally accidentally I assure you. Here goes:

Saturday night, dinner for two,
A table by the wall,
Conversing esoterically
Gazing deeply into your eyes
A quiet, idyllic dinner.
Waiting patiently at the corner
of my plate
the incredible diving potato.

We spoke of creation
and mental control
We spoke of our dreams
and we shared our goals
and we were close to each other
until the incredible diving potato
stole the show.

I finished the meat
Just the gravy remained
A pool in the center of my plate.
As I picked the potato up

with my fork
I started to share how I felt
My words they were flowing
My aura was glowing
I was clearly outdoing myself
Until the incredible diving potato
Upstaged me.

It did a two and one-half complete turn backflip
into the gravy pool:
EXPLOSION,
gravy sprayed on everything
And all I could say was
'He earned a perfect 10.'
You laughed hysterically
And my feet got nervous and
started to leave without me.

I've met some very famous men
in my day -
Barack Obama, Paul Harvey,
Alice Cooper. Daniel Condron,
An old train bandit,
But the story I love to tell
is of the incredible diving potato.

I ate him anyway."

Lynda smiled and said, "That is something I expected to hear
from you, and I enjoyed it very much. More?"

"Yes, but this one I never planned to publish even after I am a well-read writer.

when i consider
i shudder
it is not for me to say
only to pay
why what when and how
we know not yet
if it should ever
more likely never. the end

"Here is another I will never publish. As a matter of fact, you are the first person ever to hear it.

once upon a time there was. as it grew alteration set in.
at last it reached the point where it fully achieved.
however time does not permit glorying in achieving
and shortly thereafter it no longer was.
could the altered memory and records cause
true eternal survival? rather, with each
retelling, the being telling altered that
which he told, until although it still was, it
itself no longer existed. time had achieved
its victory. once upon a time there was.

"That is all that I brought with me. Do you think I have any potential?"
"Yes, you do. I am tired so let's go to bed now. See you at breakfast. Sleep well. I love you."

"I love you, too. I love you more."

As he went to bed Brad felt different. He had shared all of his poems with someone other than Jerry.

Lynda Stays the Night

Lynda was now regularly coming by Aunt Millie's every night on her way home from work. She would play cards with the three of them, give Jerry a massage, or just sit in the kitchen with ice cream, coffee, and conversation. Then about 10:05 it was time for Jerry to go to bed and she would leave and drive the short mile home. After doing this for three *w*eeks she told Millie she would like to sleep over in her room sometimes, her parents were fine with that, and her work was within walking distance of the B&B so she wouldn't need to use her car. Millie was delighted to have her stay. The first week she stayed five nights, the nights before she would go to work at the café. That meant driving over on Monday night and walking back to the B&B five evenings after work. Brad asked her to dinner the two nights the café was closed so she drove to Millie's arriving before five p.m. those nights and the two went out in his car dining at her two favorite restaurants in Piggott, one each night. Jerry joined them on Sundays, but they dined alone on Mondays. Millie said it was no problem for her to cook something for Jerry each Monday.

Because Brad and Jerry were stamp collectors, Lynda offered to take them to the post office. On the wall above the door to the postmaster's office there was a WPA mural. They didn't tell her they had already been to the post office a couple of times. The following Monday Lynda came over early and the three of them walked over to the post office and viewed the mural for some twenty minutes before purchasing commemorative stamps to use on the postcards and notes they sent to family and friends. The mural was famous and showed a twin propeller airplane with two men loading mail bags onto the plane. On the ground the pilot stood next to a mail carrier in uniform who was receiving a letter from a young man. Brad took several pictures of the mural from every angle he could. After they walked about for a short while, they went back to the B&B. Jerry stayed for dinner with Millie. Brad and Lynda went out for their once-a-week private dinner.

Three weeks after Lynda began staying over five nights a week, she told Millie she would like to spend the night sleeping next to Brad. That had been his desire and she had decided it was a good idea. She promised Millie since Jerry was in a bed two feet away from them nothing improper would happen. Millie was fine with that. She loved Lynda and wanted her to be happy and Lynda seemed happiest when with the Oak Park boys. She also knew Lynda was beginning to think she would marry Brad and the better they knew each other the easier her decision would be. They agreed not to tell Lynda's parents about the new arrangement. It only took one week before Brad became a little more aggressive and Lynda didn't say no. They assumed Jerry was asleep, but asleep or not he did not mention anything. So, Tuesday, Thursday and Saturday become sex nights. That meant Lynda was only home with her parents on Sunday night. One night the two of them were nearly rocking the bed and sighing loud enough that they now were sure Jerry was on to what was occurring. Still, he said nothing, and he seemed quite happy just to have Lynda massage his leg and his back every other night with Brad doing it every other night and also on Sundays.

Lynda left early every Sunday to go to church with her parents. After breakfast one Sunday she asked Jerry, "Why did you stop going to church?"

Jerry answered, "Two weeks after my fiancée broke up with me, I went to church and sat in the balcony. Looking down I saw Barbara sitting close to her new boyfriend and when we sang hymns, I could hear her voice separate from all the rest. I couldn't concentrate on the sermon as I kept looking at her and our breakup was running through my head. If only I had said something different. If only I had called her the day before. I was tortured so badly I almost began to cry. The next week I sat in the back of the balcony where I couldn't possibly see them, and I sang loud and didn't hear her voice. It went so well I got in line to shake the minister's hand. Almost as I reached him, they walked past me holding hands and laughing softly, just as she used to do with me. That night Brad and I went out for a beer, and he advised me not to go back."

"Why? What did he say?"

"You tell her Brad."

"Well, I thought self-torture was foolish. So, I said his life was like that of a man who wanted to take a short cut and climb through a large hole in a wire fence. The first day he went slowly headfirst through the hole and unfortunately touched the wire with his left arm and leg. He had two long

91

bleeding scratches. The next day he decided to jump through quickly but to aim just a bit to the right of last time. He landed on the other side with three long scratches on his right side and leg. The third time he decided to go deliberately slow. Head through okay, left arm through okay, upper torso through okay. But then he felt the wires touching his butt, so he backed out slowly and never took that short cut again. It wasn't worth it."

"Good argument, but I wouldn't compare praising God to taking a short cut."

"I said if church was important to him, he should move down the street to the Methodist Church for the next year or so."

"Instead of that Brad and I just stopped going to church," Jerry said.

"Being a metaphysician, he made a weird sort of Presbyterian anyway."

"Will you two come to church with me next week?"

"Yes, I will," Jerry said.

"Sure," Brad said.

"What does sure mean in this context? Only because I have to?"

"Something like that. You know I love you and I want to do what you want me to do as long as it doesn't compromise my core values."

"Which are?"

"I think you know by now. All persons are my brothers and sisters. We are all part of the same creative force which moves life on Earth. Love is the most important thing and we all must love everyone no matter what happens."

"Even evil persons like Hitler or Stalin?"

"Absolutely. Love the sinner but not the sin. Pray for your enemies. And all violence is wrong. So never hurt anyone physically for any reason no matter what. And never hurt them emotionally if that is possible."

Lynda looked hurt. "So, some brute is punching me, and you would not defend me?"

"Of course, I would. I would step between the two of you and make him stop hitting you."

"So now he punches you in the eye. You just take it?"

"Correct. I would tell him to take it easy. Most violent people are caught by surprise when you don't punch back, and so far, none has hit me a second time. In college freshman year our roommate once hit me in the face as hard as he could. We had been wrestling on the floor and I pushed him away because I wanted to stop wrestling and go watch television. I had forgotten he had blown up a test tube the summer before college and his body was still passing out small pieces of glass on occasion. He said I punched him, but that was never my intention. and the push was definitely not a punch."

"So, then what?"

"My face really hurt for a good long time and not like any pain I had ever felt before. I simply said, 'Take it easy Jack' and walked away. I returned to our room and missed the show *Seinfeld*. About seven of us watched it every weekday lunch hour on the television in our dorm lounge. In my room I took off my glasses and marveled how he could have landed a punch on my upper cheek and not knocked off my glasses or even broken them. Two hours later still hurting, I walked to my class. Three days later my face didn't hurt anymore and that felt strange for a few minutes."

"So, you have never punched anyone?" Lynda said.
"Only once. My cousin Jim and I are about the same age. We had walked out into the woods. I didn't understand it, but he kept demanding I fight with him. He stood in front of me so I couldn't walk away. Finally, I swung my fist softly and hit him in the nose. His nose started bleeding and the fight was over. We walked home as much friends as ever, but I felt like shit having caused his nose to bleed.

"The next time I didn't get into a fight I was working at the insurance company. The guy next to me became a pretty good friend and told me lots of personal things. He was living with a beautiful girl and told me he loved her a lot. Nevertheless, driving down the street one time he passed a cute girl driving and put his hand up to his mouth 'Want to have a drink with me?' She nodded yes and they went into the next bar together. I'm not sure what all they did but I know his hands wandered over her body some. Then a few weeks later his girlfriend called me at work. 'I think he is cheating on me and I am going to kick him out of my apartment, but to be totally sure I am doing the right thing, can you confirm my suspicions?' I now was forced to hurt someone. Lie and I hurt her because she remains with a guy who cheats on her. Tell the truth and I hurt him. I chose to tell the truth. The truth always wins. So, I told her about the girl in the car. I am sure she was not the only girl he picked up while living with his girlfriend. The next Friday night he and I are in a bar having a few. Suddenly he turns on me and asks 'Why did you tell on me? She just kicked me out of her apartment.' Before I could say a thing, he hit me in the stomach as hard as he could. I pushed his shoulders gently to create a space between us, turned, and walked out of the bar. Somehow I managed to not throw up and after resting in my locked car about ten minutes I drove home."

"Some would think you are a coward."

"They can think that if they wish. The only person whose thoughts I can control is myself. The only actions I can control are my own."

After Church

Walking home from church the next Sunday, Brad asked, "Have you ever actually heard the voice of God?"

Lynda said, "Yes, I have. Several times in a dream He has spoken to me, given me answers to important questions I had prayed about."

Brad replied, "One night I talked to Ernest Hemingway in a dream."

"Are you making fun of me?"

"No, not at all. It is just I see God as a creator of all things seen and unseen, a field of all possibilities as Deepak Chopra writes. God is not male, female, trans, bisexual, nonsexual, young, or old. He is all knowing, all seeing, all being, all not in the physical but a spiritual being. Yet the creator is in everything in the universe, in every molecule and in every part of each of us. I think the church has made the creator into a male figure while I think of him as that still small voice within me. I think you heard that still small voice which some call your conscience."

"Jesus called him father. Father is male," Lynda said with authority.

Seeing Brad was not responding, she then said, "Okay. So, what did your Hemingway say to you?"

"For the last ten years if anyone asked me if I could go back in time where and when would I go, my reply was always 'I would be with Ernest Hemingway at dinner in the Finca Vigia, his home in Cuba. He was so learned, so well read, such a great listener, and always had a sense of humor. I think conversation over dinner would be the best thing I could ever experience."

"Until you got drunk and passed out. I asked what did he say to you?"

"In dreams time and space don't have to mesh. My Hemingway, as you just called him, was about 37 years old and had a mustache. I was probably my current age, not so much younger than him. He came to Oak Park to talk to us docents, the ones who give tours of his birth house. He sat down on the back side of a long row of tables, and we filed in one at a time. I was really disappointed that my chair was one past the chair directly across from him. The person behind me would sit directly across from him and thus have the best opportunity to talk to him. Suddenly the tables split apart, and he and I were across from each other, and I didn't notice anyone else. We were alone. He spoke directly to me. He said, 'I got a damn 60-dollar parking ticket on my car today!' I replied 'Oak Park is famous for its parking tickets. I have had several I questioned but they always make me pay. It is in their budget, nearly $1 million income every year from parking tickets. We call Oak Park 'No Park.' Just at that moment my cat woke me up to give her her breakfast."

"Great conversation."

"Yea, it was about to be. I often meditate and invite him back, but he hasn't returned yet. Even more than fifty some years after his death he is still in great demand. I expect him to come back to me at a time of his own choosing. Sort of like when my Mercedes found me."

The following week there was another conversation of Lynda's god versus Brad's creator.

Brad said "I do not see God as a him or a her, or anything like a human. Rather I see our creator as loving energy, which is omnipotent, omnipresent, unbounded by time, space, or by physicality. It is like the pure light we cannot reproduce while in the physical. It contains the field of all possibilities and everything that ever existed or will exist, and it is not confined by time and space as we are."

Lynda sounded annoyed when she answered "God is our father. Jesus is his only begotten son. The Bible is the clear word of God as He wrote through his son's disciples."

"Have you read the whole Bible?" Brad asked.

"God is love; God smote the enemies of the Jewish people. God sent plagues to Egypt to destroy their food supply, kill their first-born sons, drown their armies. Love would not do that."

"That is the Old Testament."

"Revolutions is in the New Testament. It is about blood baths. I read it as a dream and not as the direct word of God. Every person in your dream is an aspect of yourself. Unless someone from beyond the grave appears to talk to you. In that case the mouth of the person moves as he talks. John wrote Revelations after a weird dream which he gave God credit for sending to him."

"I believe on judgment day God will rise up the righteous to Heaven and he will destroy the sinners by sending them to Hell."

"Loving God?'

"A just God. Heaven must be earned. God's grace must be earned."

"Hemingway's father believed that, and he never wasted a minute of his time but was always doing something productive. That contributed to his need to leave his family and go on rest cures. Relaxation is a critical part of life."

At that point they decided to go into the kitchen and get a drink. They could see that when this conversation ended, they would be in two separate places.

The following Monday when Lynda arrived at Aunt Millie's, Brad was aløne in the kitchen singing out loud while washing dishes. The song he sang was *Sunday Morning Coming Down* by Kris Kristofferson as sung by Johnny Cash. It was Brad's favorite song.

Lynda walked into the kitchen, he stopped singing, and she asked him "Why do you sing so many songs of loss and loneliness?"

"They are some of the best tunes and have the most moving words." Brad said. "I love Johnny Cash, so I sing many of his songs."

"Johnny Cash again. Yea, I know all about that. So, sing me one of his hymns."

Brad finished washing the mixing bowl, set down the washing sponge, got Lynda a cup of coffee, and then began to sing, *I call him*.

I think Johnny actually wrote that hymn. Some relative named Roy, I believe he was Johnny's brother, helped him with the lyrics."

"That was nice. A few flat notes perhaps, but nice. I am happy you started coming to church with me."

"I am too, but not many ministers like to discuss reincarnation with me."

"Just keep your opinions to yourself. Just say 'Good sermon' as we shake his hand and leave."

"Okay. I've been good so far, haven't I? And without Barbara, Jerry is happy to be going to church again too."

"Speaking of Barbara, how long after she broke it off with him was his accident?"

"It was four weeks to the day."

"Was it really accidental or did he do it on purpose?"

"That I cannot say. Only he can. He maintains it was an accident."

"And do you believe him?"

"That I cannot say."

Helping Millie

Brad had set up their stay with Millie at a reduced rate in exchange for helping her with chores. One such chore was to do the laundry he and Jerry created. He would strip their beds twice a week and carry the sheets and pillowcases into the laundry room. He also took all their dirty clothes and pajamas and put them into the wash too. Then he cleaned the laundry room. Lynda walked in on him one Monday and saw him picking tiny pieces of lint and dirt off the floor and putting them into the waste basket.

"Why don't you use a broom?" she inquired.
"He can't. It is not in the agreement."
"Who can't? What agreement?"
"The German prisoner. It is a game I play to motivate me to do a thorough job. I pretend I am a Jewish prisoner in Germany in 1944. Colonel Schmidt took me to his home to do all the menial tasks for him. He told me if I picked up enough dirt and lint to fill his waste basket before February 1945, he would not shoot me. If I failed to clean well enough or to fill the waste basket I would be shot in the back yard on March first. One of his soldiers kicked over the waste basket in January and so he extended my deadline until May 1945. In April the Americans liberated me so I moved to America, and

he came over as a prisoner of war. Then I gave him the same deal he had given me. Fill the waste basket by hand before September 1946 and you can go to München for Oktoberfest. If the waste basket is not full, I dump it out and you have another year to try to get to Oktoberfest."

"Is München Munich"

"Ja. I spent a couple of weeks in a German Apartment when I attended Oktoberfest three years ago, and I learned to use the German name for many things, but mostly München, my German Heimat Stadt – home-town."

"Did anyone ever tell you that you are weird?"

"Not until you did. Thank you for informing me."

"I'll be in the kitchen when Herr Schmidt finishes his job."

"Now you get the idea. Oh, by the way, I don't call myself weird, I call myself a gradualist."

"Like how your novel is being written?"

"Yes. I have written about 100 notes to self to use when I find time to write."

"If you want to skip dinner tonight to write, just say so. Jerry and I can eat with Aunt Millie while you write."

"Not on your life mine *Schatzie*. We have a dinner date like every *Montag*."

"OK. But start writing soon or stop calling yourself a writer. And stop with the German already."

As Lynda went into the kitchen, she heard Brad singing *Die Liechtensteiner Polka.*

Looking back, she saw him picking up a bit of cat hair off the floor and dropping it gingerly into his liberation waste basket.

Then as she walked nearly out of earshot she heard

Bier hier, Bier hier, oder ich fall um, juchhe!
Bier hier, Bier hier, oder ich fall um!
Soll das Bier im Keller liegen
Und ich hier die Ohnmacht kriegen?
Bier hier, Bier hier, oder ich fall um!

A week earlier Lynda had asked Millie if she could bring her cat Furball to stay with them since she spent nearly all of her time there and her brother Billy was tired of taking care of Furball six and a half days out of seven. Millie said of course she could, but the cat wasn't to go into her room. Also, Brad was to vacuum three times a week instead of twice as originally agreed to. Yesterday Billy had told Lynda that a neighbor had brought home a stray Beagle mix and no one on their block wanted the dog. He feared the dog would be put down. Could she take it? She said no, but Brad said he would take it. After he finished folding the laundry and vacuuming the dining room and the common room, the two of them and Jerry would drive over and meet the dog. Brad finished at 3:30 and they got into his car and drove over to Lynda's parents neighbor to meet the stray dog. Brad and Lynda held hands as they walked up to the door. The door was opened by an overweight man dressed in baggy pants held up with suspenders and wearing a flannel shirt with obvious stains on it. He opened the door about two minutes after they first rang the doorbell. A cigar looking as if it weren't lit hung from his lips.

"Here for the mutt, Lynda?" he asked.

"Yes, we are" Brad replied.

"He might have fleas."

"Can we just see him please."

When the man returned, he held an underfed beagle mix who looked like an unbrushed and unfed tramp.

"I'll take him," Brad said immediately. He took him from the man's arms, thanked the man for rescuing the poor dog, and turned to walk to the car. Lynda stayed at the door and talked to her old neighbor for a few minutes, and Jerry remained with her. When they finally got in the car Brad was petting the dog and the dog was howling but in a way that almost sounded like singing.

"Meet Mr. Johnny Cash," he said to Jerry and Lynda. "He sings beautifully, don't you think?'

"He needs a bath," Lynda said.

"You can't use that name," Jerry said. "It's already taken."

"My dog, my name," Brad replied. Then after a few moments of thought, "Meet Mr. JR Cash."

"I'll call him JR," Jerry said.

"Guess I'll call him Mr. Cash," Lynda said.

Brad started the engine and slowly pulled out into the street still petting his new dog with his right hand while steering with his left one. Lynda said both hands on the wheel please and as he removed his hand from JR's head, Mr. Cash put his chin on Brad's thigh for the ride back home.

Before going to work the next afternoon, and after bathing Mr. Cash in the laundry tub, Brad went to the local vet to give his dog a checkup. Mr. Cash was basically fine, no worms and no fleas. Brad bought an organic bag of grain free dry dog food and he and Mr. Cash sang *I Walk the Line* on the way home. Millie again said not in my room, but your dog is welcome everywhere else in the house unless the other room is rented to someone else, and they don't like dogs. In that case keep him in your room. The dog dishes for food and water were placed out of the walking path near a seldom used cabinet in the kitchen. Furball immediately claimed the water dish and Mr. Cash politely waited until she had left before coming over to drink. Furball also tasted the dog food but left after eating only three bites. Having again watched quietly while waiting his turn, Mr. Cash then came up to his food dish and ate every last bit with obvious pleasure. Food placed in his dish twice a day barely touched by Furball, this was like heaven for him. At night he slept on Brad's feet and once or twice squeezed between Brad and Lynda, but each time she shooed him back to the foot of the bed.

"I prefer a man touching me to a dog pushing me away," she said.

"I'm glad. I love you and I love you next to me," he replied.

Brad then said another prayer to the God he wasn't sure he believed in. "Thank you, dear God. I have found my soul mate, the true love I always hoped to find. Jerry is starting to walk better and is becoming the old Jerry again. And to add honey to my life I get a stray dog to love and from whom I will receive unconditional love. Mr. Cash fills any tiny need I still had. Aunt Millie is closer to me than either of my real aunts. About the only thing I need now is to find more ways to give back. See what you can do. Amen." And then he sang in his thoughts

Amen, amen
Amen, amen, amen
Amen, amen
Amen, amen, amen
See the little baby, amen
Wrapped in a manger, amen
On Christmas morning, amen, amen amen
See Him in the temple, amen
Talking with the elders, amen

Who marveled at His wisdom, amen, amen, amen
Amen, amen,
Amen, amen, amen

He forgot the next verse, but surely God wouldn't care if he only knew some of the words. It wasn't like he was in the church choir or anything important like that.

Environment

The kitchen in the B&B had just added a coffee maker which made one cup at a time. Millie let the guests choose from about six different types of coffee. Wait for the coffee maker to read ready to brew, add the little plastic cup with coffee grounds, push medium or large cup button, and when finished walk away with a hot cup of coffee. Next person puts the used plastic cup into the trash, inserts his choice, and repeats as desired. Brad made his cup of French Roast coffee but didn't like throwing away the used plastic cup. He decided to save the used ones for one day, tear the tops off and dump the used coffee grounds into a plastic bucket which he then dumped in the yard for compost.

Stopping at the grocery store on the way home from work that night he bought everything on his shopping list and added two new items, plastic reusable cups for the coffee machine and a small bag of ground coffee beans to use with his reusable cups. The grounds would still be compostable, but then the cup would be washed out and reused.

Lynda asked him why he did that.

"They found a patch of plastic floating in the Pacific Ocean bigger than Arkansas," he replied.

He wasn't sure it was bigger than Arkansas, but since he was in Arkansas, he used that state and assumed no one else would be certain either.

"I decided to use as little plastic as I can to help reduce the problem."

"Two plastic cups a day won't make any difference."

"True. What if all four of us do this? Now it amounts to eight a day. What if every person in Arkansas did this? Twelve million fewer plastic cups every day."

"That is never going to happen."

"So, what if 20 percent of the population do this? Still reduce the number of cups in the trash by almost two million."

"You are probably just wasting your time and money."

"Doing what is correct cannot ever be a waste of time or effort or money."

"Did anyone ever tell you that you are weird?'

"No, but thank you for that information."

Brad then explained to Lynda, every evening back home in Oak Park two hours before bedtime he walked down the basement stairs to fetch a bottle of beer, but he never turned on the basement light. When he opened the refrigerator and took out his beer, the refrigerator light came on. When he walked back upstairs, he could see a bit from light coming from the neighbor's house. Lynda naturally asked him,

"Why do you go downstairs in the dark?'

"Electricity generation contributes to global warming."

"What if you fall down the stairs in the dark?"

"Won't happen. I count nine steps, turn to my left, count three more and then feel the floor beneath my feet. I can see a tiny bit from that point on because a bit of light from the streetlight comes through the window. When I open the refrigerator door a light comes on and I select my beer and come back upstairs."

"And open the bottle in the dark!"

"Yes, actually I do. The last drawer on the right of one cabinet, first wooden handle on the left side is my bottle opener."

"Did anyone ever tell you that you are weird?"

"No, you are the first and only one. And more than one time actually."

"One more question," she asked. "Why do you remove the labels from cans before you recycle them."

"Two different processes. Recycle aluminum, recycle paper. If I leave the labels on the cans, I expect they just burn them off at the recycle plant."

"And that small amount of paper matters because?"

"Because if 20 percent of the people did this, we would recycle millions of additional pieces of paper."

"What else do you do to save the planet?"

"Hum." Brad thought for a few moments. Lynda knew that a long list would be coming.

He began, "I turn off the car engine while waiting for freight trains to pass. When going to the bank and the post office in Oak Park I park at the bank, walk to the post office, then walk back to my car at the bank, thus saving one start and one stop and about 1/3 of a mile of driving. I look for locally sourced food in the grocery store. When you eat an apple, you cut off four sides and leave a square core. Before I compost it, I eat some apple from each of the four cuts. Waste not, want not. I compost all of our coffee grounds.

"At home I always take the train to downtown Chicago and never drive downtown. On trips I leave town before or after the rush hour. I turn the thermostat down just three degrees at night and when I will be away from home more than three hours. In the summer I do the same with the air conditioning, turn the temp up at night and when I will be away from home more than four hours. I only use real silverware which is reusable and never use plastic, real drinking glasses and never paper or plastic cups, cloth napkins and not paper ones. I grow my own tomatoes, Swiss Chard, potatoes in a barrel, peppers, mint, onions, and flowers. I hold you close on a cold night, so we don't have to turn up the thermostat."
Lynda's response, "Did anyone ever tell you that you are a little weird?"
"Only you, but I love you for it."
"I love you too, but still think you are a little weird."

"Better weird than boring. Better weird than mean. Better weird than lazy. Better weird than selfish."

"Alright already."

"Oh, I also support several animal welfare groups with a monthly donation, they range from the Animal Care League in Oak Park to the ASPCA and other dog and cat rescue charities, two big cat rescue ranches, lions, tigers, cheetahs and the like, and also African Wildlife Foundation. We need to save animals in order to save ourselves.

"Probably more important, I support trees and other plants. Arbor Day, Nature Conservancy, Morton Arboretum, California Redwoods, and so on. I don't have any grass in our front yard but have everything from flowers to herbs to tomato plants to holly bushes and other blooming bushes. Our yard is a certified wildlife habitat. We have hummingbirds, cardinals, sparrows, finches, opossums, skunks, an occasional raccoon and even a very rare visit by a deer, rare because the Thatcher Woods are over four miles away. We even have a hawk who visits us about once a week. Of course, then all the other birds hide as best as they can. Recently coyotes have returned to Oak Park and a few foxes as well. And Jerry and I own a lake lot at a man-made lake. We quit going there when they banned camping on our own lot, but we kept it undeveloped so the trees remain and the lot remains a place to reduce carbon from the air."

"Seems a waste of money to pay assessments and taxes and not use the land," Lynda said.

"They have a corn boil each fall and a ten k race each spring and we sometimes drive down for one or both of those activities."

"You run ten k races?" she asked.

"We used to run a lot, but now just that one. I take about an hour to run the 6.2 miles and Jerry takes about 53 minutes. I should say he used to take 53 minutes. With what the accident did to his right leg, I am not sure he will run any more races. Maybe now we will just walk. I had forgotten about our long walks. In the Boy Scouts we both earned the hiking merit badge. That was five hikes with a minimum of twenty miles or more each. Our most fun one was the Lincoln Trail from New Salem to Springfield. Our troop joined two other troops that day and they had us start two boys at a time every minute or so. Jerry and I were the third from the last pair to start and the first pair had about an hour head start on us. He bet me we could pass them by the halfway mark of thirteen miles and I agreed we could. We started jogging and passed pair after pair without slowing down. I think we ran for two hours when we caught the second pair who didn't want to let us pass them, so they started sprinting. We sped up and tried to stay close to them and after about ten minutes they gave up. By then we were far ahead of everyone as the front pair only ran for about two minutes. Don't hold me to this as it was almost twenty years ago, but I seem to remember running the entire twenty-six-mile trail. Of course, the last thirteen were a much slower jog once we were in the lead."

When he paused for a breath Lynda decided to get them coffee and cookies, thinking he might go all night. Brad always loved coffee and cookies, cakes, pies, and or ice cream so he walked into the kitchen with her and made his own coffee.

Back in the common room he resumed his story. "We arrived in Springfield more than an hour and forty-five minutes before our scoutmaster did. We looked at the state capitol building and then walked about. In front of one hotel a large man pushed us both backwards about three feet. We looked past him to see why, and some Saudi Arabian prince got out of a limo and went into the hotel. Even pushed back we were almost close enough to touch him, but of course the bodyguard next to us would never have permitted that to happen."

"Keep on talking now that I have my coffee," Lynda said.

"Sorry, guess I was off topic, but I am amazed looking back how determined we were to finish first and how we then just kept running a full marathon. Only time in my life I ever ran that far, and I assure you I couldn't do that today. Actually, I couldn't do it again in my mid-twenties until some girl at work who I had started to date told me she loved to run five k and ten k races. So, I told Jerry I wanted to run, and he joined me in training. First day we jogged around our block. Next two days around two blocks. Next three days around three blocks. We worked up to about three and a half miles in a half hour. Then we ran our first ten k with Betty. Jerry pulled ahead of us in order to finish in 54 minutes. She and I finished in 59 minutes 59 seconds. When she got her breath enough to talk, she said to me that that had been her fastest ten k ever. I told her I was just keeping up with her. She said she was just keeping up with me. Then we quit running and took up skiing."

Brad drank half his cup of coffee and ate two cookies. "So go ahead and tell me about your skiing," Lynda said after she also drank half a cup and ate one cookie.

"Her ski club was the BUCS. Two of my other friends from work were also members so I joined, too. We skied locally and up at Boyne City in northern Michigan. We found out the club's name meant barely under control skiers, so I fit in perfectly. I was no longer dating Betty when the club took a bus to Winter Park, Colorado. Talk about mountain skiing, that was my first time. The run Mary Jane was said to be the hardest run, full of moguls and small jumps, so I decided to try it first. After all I knew how to spread my skis and sit down when I needed an emergency stop. I had a lot of fun and only sat down about two dozen times. The others later told me it was best not to ski alone, but to always have one other club member with you just in case. End of ski story. I just ran down twice and then stopped for hot rum in the hut café."

"Do you ski?" he asked Lynda.
"I thought you'd never ask. I do but am really a bunny hill and easy run kind of skier. I don't want to hit a tree or break a leg."
"Fair enough. We'll ski next winter a few times. I am tired now and tomorrow is a workday so let's make out a bit and go to bed."
Lynda kissed him a few times, a little rubbing and squeezing, and a long, good night kiss. They fell asleep shortly after getting into bed.

Come to Oak Park

Brad had decided Lynda was the woman for him, so he decided to let her know just how great Oak Park was. Do I start with 'when we are married' no 'when you come to Oak Park' no 'the great things about living in Oak Park' sure.

"The things Jerry and I love most about Oak Park are the things that we believe make it the greatest village in the world. Number one for me are the Hemingway Archives and the Hemingway Birth House and the Hemingway Boyhood Home and even the interim house where he lived while the boyhood house was being built. Of course, I volunteered at the birth house almost every other weekend. The foundation spent more than ten years and over one and a quarter million dollars making the house look like it looked when Ernest lived there in 1899 to 1905. I love that we have visitors from just about every country in the world. Sometimes they stay and talk to me after the tour, and I answer questions and find out more about them. Often visitors from France and Germany, England and Australia give me their addresses and tell me to look them up next time I go to Europe or Australia."

"Have you ever contacted any of them afterwards?" she said.

"Yes, but we, Jerry and I, haven't been to anywhere where it would be convenient to contact one of them in person. Jerry also gave tours for a few years before he decided it wasn't really his thing. Before his accident he gave tours at the Frank Lloyd Wright Home and Studio. I have contacted one German lady by mail. When she found out I collected German stamps she told me she had her father's stamp collection and was ready to give it away. We wrote two letters each and then she mailed me his collection. Also, one man from Australia sent me information on the Hall family in Australia. Oh, that is because Hemingway's grandfather was Ernest Hall, hence he thought there might be a connection between the Halls there and Ernie's family in Oak Park."

"Was there?"

"I don't know. I don't have time to do genealogy, but I hope to find out someday. They both were originally from England. But back to why we love Oak Park, I mentioned Frank Lloyd Wright. We have more homes that he designed than any other community in the world. Also, Unity Temple, a masterpiece he designed for the Unitarians' new church. He did it on a very tight budget. The current church, in conjunction with the Frank Lloyd Wright Association, has spent far more maintaining it than was spent building it. We have a tour called Wright Plus every year and Jerry and I stand in one house on the tour and give a short talk to the people coming through. That way we get to tour all eight or nine houses

122

the Friday evening before the big tour on Saturday. We get thousands of people from all over the country in Oak Park for that tour.

"Oak Park also has a Symphony Orchestra, rather good if I do say so myself. Jerry and I have season tickets and get to attend a reception for season ticket holders in one of Oak Park's finest houses each year. The concerts are in one of our many older churches along Lake Street."

"I would like to go to those."

"You will when you are in Oak Park. Next, we used to have the oldest Community Lecture Series in the country. My parents attended most of them and I would have gone had they not discontinued them before I graduated from high school. Many famous and important people came to lecture."

"Name one."

"The movie critic for the Chicago Tribune. At that time, it was Roger Ebert. In earlier times I think people like Jane Addams and Amelia Erhardt came, as well as politicians from both Illinois and national.

"We also have a conservatory with plants from all over the world. We have a century plant there and when it blooms, once each century I believe, it will require some glass to be removed from the roof of the greenhouse as it will shoot up so tall it cannot be contained under the roof.

"Next we had the Oak Park Council on International Affairs. We were the oldest group in the country which was set up to support the Peace Corps. 'Mrs. Oak Park,' Elsie Jacobsen, went to Washington, D.C. when President Kennedy started the Peace Corps. She met Sargant Schreiber and said I am an old lady and don't plan to go overseas so what can I do to help. They created the School-to-School program. Oak Park grade school classes created and sent packages to villages where the Peace Corps was building a school. The students who received the packages sent drawings and thank you notes back to the Oak Park kids. That evolved into the Peace Corps Partnership Program. We partnered with a Peace Corps volunteer, and we sent $1,000 per project to projects set up by Peace Corps volunteers. Some now are asking for more than a thousand dollars, but we still sent one thousand and only partially fund more expensive projects. Four years ago, Jerry and I paid for a school in the hills of Guatemala. They told us the natives cried when they heard they had been selected for a school."

"Bet that made you feel good."

"It sure did. Very good. Jerry and I also went to the annual dinner to raise money for our council. Oak Park CIA built about 1,000 projects working with Peace Corps volunteers. We paid for the dinner and then donated an extra fifty dollars each for the projects. As we left, we bought a table decoration plant which was donated by the Oak Park Conservatory and that raised another $10 each."

"What Church did you go to in Oak Park?" Lynda asked.

"Jerry went to the First Presbyterian Church. My parents belong to the First Baptist Church. I was baptized there and attended until about three years ago. Some years ago, the First Presbyterian Church and First Congregational Church merged to form the First United Church of Oak Park. Jerry went there in what had been the Congregational church building. I attended there with him a dozen or so times, but then I stopped going to any church. We can expand on this later.

"Back to what we love about Oak Park. We have an Infant Welfare Society. They provide health and other services to infants, mostly from lower income families. We have an Orphanage, Hephzibah Children's Home. Dr. Hemingway was one of the doctors for the orphans in the late 1890s up until sometime in the 19 teens. I took a tour there once with a friend who was visiting Oak Park and it is a wonderful home. Maybe someday my wife and I will be a foster home for an orphan until he or she gets adopted."

"I would prefer to raise children if I was their mother," Lynda said.

"It is hard to adopt a troubled child," Brad continued, "But I always believed it was the right thing to do if you have the means and the disposition. An aside. I went to an adoption agency when I turned thirty because I realized I might never get married. They didn't laugh at me but said I would never get any healthy baby or young child. Those went to married couples. So, they said I could probably get the young boy who had Spina Bifida and was learning impaired and would probably never think better than a fourth grader. I couldn't do that because I would have had to pay a full-time nurse while I was at work and that made no sense. A family with a stay-at-home parent should adopt him, not a single man. When I told Jerry he refused to quit his job and stay home so that ended without any more meetings."

"Why would Jerry stay home and not you?"

"At that time, I was earning a few thousand dollars more than him and a family of three needed all of that income and probably even a bit more."

Brad continued, "Oak Park also has the Cappelli Institute of Music. Our youth learn to sing. After 1896 Grace Hemingway was the music teacher in Oak Park, but today they go to Cappelli and learn a great deal about music. Oak Park has a wonderful art studio too, the Oak Park Art League. Grace Hemingway sold her paintings there after she quit teaching music. I used to believe she was even a co-founder of the Art League, but it turns out the league was nearly fifty years old when she joined. I believe she sold over 700 paintings through the Art League and the cost even then was at least $100 each.

"Then we have a recently revived historical society. It was upstairs in one room of the Farson-Mills House until a stand-alone building on Lake Street was constructed in an old firehouse. The Farson-Mills house is also known as Pleasant Home because the two streets which meet at that corner are Pleasant street and Home avenue. Today it belongs to the park district as does another amazing mansion, the Cheny Mansion. When you come up, we'll go there too as it is an unbelievable house. Sits on a full city block and has a green house and outdoor gardens and a gardener's cottage. I have been to several events there and Jerry and I have gone on the guided tour of the house. I will go back in an instant any time I can."

"Oak Park is known for its architecture, isn't it?' Lynda asked.
"Yes, from Italianate to Victorian to Frank Lloyd Wright to E.E. Roberts to a solar house to modern houses, which are not so great in my opinion. One being built now they claim will be energy independent and totally off the grid.

"For almost a century Oak Park was dry and was known as the village where taverns stop and churches begin. Pius people called it 'Saints Rest.' You might enjoy visiting our churches to see the architecture there too. I believe there are still over twenty-five churches. Not too long ago the Hemingway Museum was on the first floor of what used to be a church. A very wealthy woman bought the church when the congregation became too small to support it. She made it into a community center. She rented the first floor to the Oak Park Hemingway Society. But now the sanctuary upstairs is once again used as a church, and they got the Hemingway Museum to pack up and move out. Our beautiful museum is packed up and in storage.

"To wrap up, Oak Park has excellent schools, both grade schools and our high school. Both of Hemingway's parents went to Oak Park-River Forest High as did he and his five siblings, my parents, Jerry's mother, Jerry, and me. Our children will go there, too. I see one of them being a very successful writer, painter, poet, musician, or politician. I'm hoping for writer. River Forest, our sister village, has two universities. Two! River Forest has both Dominican University and Concordia University. They allow adults to sit in on some classes for a very nominal fee. We could take a few classes if you like."

Money Talk

The next Monday at dinner Lynda brought up money.

"You say we are going to be married and live in your house in Oak Park."

"Yes. And we will be happy as two bugs in a rug. Two lovers in a sleeping bag. Two wolves eating a deer they just caught."

"How will we pay the taxes? The car insurance? Gas? Buy clothes for me to wear to work? Feed Furball and Mr. Cash? Drive down to Piggott to visit my family?"

"I will get my old job back at the insurance company. I earned over $48,000 a year when I took my leave."

"Yes, but you sold 30 shares of stock to come here, and that money is gone. You just got a dividend from your stock account and that money is gone. You owe the vet over $50. Aunt Millie is waiting for this week's rent on our room which was due yesterday. We are low on dog food, cat food, and wine. And…"

"You don't have to worry about that stuff. When I moved to Denver to direct the School of Metaphysics there I got by. I ended up getting up at six in the morning and doing inventory for local grocery stores. I only made $4 an hour, and it was part-time work, so I offered to drive the company van. That meant I got $4.25 an hour on days that I drove the crew to the assignment. Once we even rode all the way to Nebraska and on out-of-town trips like that, we got $2.25 an hour just for riding in the van and talking. At that time aluminum cans brought four to six cents each, so I picked up each one I walked past. Most people just tossed the cans out of the car window. If I need to, I'll find a better paying job there, but I am pretty sure we will make it on my former income and checking account balance. And if Jerry lives with us, he is earning good money too."

"I want a better life than that. You also loaned money to two of your co-workers in Denver and neither one paid you back. True?"

"True. Did Jerry tell you that? I had sold my Condo and had tens of thousands in my checking account at that time."

"As I see it you saved money for retirement. Then you quit a good job to move to Denver. There you spent your savings on living, on a school, and giving it to those who took advantage of you. Back home you got another good job. You saved for retirement and now you are spending most of that money to be here. How do I know you won't do something similar when we are married?"

"You could trust me. I would always talk it over with you before moving on to something else."

"You rented your house to your sister for the exact amount of your mortgage payment. You still need to pay the taxes and maintenance on a house you are not living in."

"True. But my sister is earning far less than I did and she is carefully saving money for a down payment on a townhouse of her own. She couldn't do that if I charged her market rate."

"You need to think of yourself more often."

"Jerry was almost killed. He needed me. Money can't be more important than friendship."

"Didn't Jerry have any savings?"

"I never asked how much, but yes he did and does."

"Perhaps you should have asked."

"Okay. Things are looking gray today, but I will call my broker, sell another few shares of stock and pay all of my bills this week."

"And have nothing left for retirement."

"Thirty or forty shares are less than one quarter of what I had. We'll be fine."

"So, your philosophy of money is spend and we'll be fine?"

"Actually, it is not quite that simple. Your mind is very powerful. If you truly believe you will be fine you will be. I think of the tithing rule. Give ten percent to charity each payday. How can you do that forever. Use the law of tenfold return. Give a charity $2, claim your right to tenfold return not for any selfish need, but so you will always have enough to give going forward."

"Does that really work for you?"

"Not always ten to one, but I always have found a way to pay my bills and have some left to give away too."

"So, when you go back to work will you put the maximum possible into your 401K?"

"Absolutely."

"And not give away any money until the balance is over $100,000?"

"That isn't the way it works. The more you give the more you receive."

"That hasn't worked for me," Lynda said decisively.

"Look, I spent maybe $6,000 coming to Piggott. Jerry has started to walk, laugh, dream, sing, and love living again. How much is that worth? You met me and fell in love with me. How much is that worth? Aunt Millie has a steady six-month income, a man to vacuum, do the laundry, weed the garden, carry any heavy things, and do her shopping. And he is one of her best friends now. How much is that worth? Six thou is a bargain if I ever saw one."

"You are right. But when we get home, I still need to write a check for my car insurance, I need money to put gas in the car, and before I can get married one of us will need a big check for my wedding dress and our reception. Mom and dad are good for only a few hundred dollars."

"We'll figure it out. I'll sell another twenty shares. Or pick up more aluminum cans."

"Then you'll have almost nothing left in your stock account. And I wish you could be more serious about things like money."

"Let me quote Ram Dass here, 'We're all just walking each other home.' And the Bible, 'Do not worry about what you shall eat or what you shall drink. Seek ye first the kingdom of God and all these things shall be added unto you.'"

As they left dinner Brad left his usual 25 percent tip. On the ride home he sang *That's where my money goes,* an olde English folk song. He was teasing Lynda, but Lynda didn't smile or think he was cute at all. Maybe a little cute, but not serious enough about financial responsibility. Money matters.

Sport Monday

At their next Monday night dinner Lynda surprised Brad by asking him about baseball.

"Jerry told me he was on the college baseball team, and you were not. He said you also weren't on the high school baseball team. Since you two are like twins how come that was true. He told me to ask you."

"Long version or short?"

"You always give the long version," she replied quickly.

"Okay. I'll start with third grade. My parents never had extra money, but they paid the fee for me to go to a baseball school. Dad was a dyed-in-the-wool Chicago Cubs fan. He was a good player and at nineteen played on their farm club. He was going to get a call up at the end of the season when he made a diving catch and broke one of his fingers. Before sports medicine that was the end of his career. Over one week before it started. He hoped I would follow in his footsteps, so he dug into his savings to pay for a baseball school for me. I was a fast runner and so I played outfield at sandlot games. Anyway, the teacher threw about fifteen pitches to each kid. I hit six of them over the cheap wire fence he had set up so every single ball I hit was a home run. No other kid did that.

135

"When I got to Oak Park High my general business teacher was the track coach and he talked me into going out for indoor track. There were two seasons, indoor track during the winter and in the spring, outdoor track. I agreed to run and ran the quarter mile mostly, half mile occasionally. Then came tryouts for baseball. Coach let Jerry go but I couldn't. I was one quarter of the mile relay race team and he let me run anchor because I missed the baseball tryouts. After that meet there were still two more weeks of indoor track. I lettered in track three years out of four but felt cheated that the coach didn't tell me indoor track meant no baseball. He loved having me on the outdoor track team anyhow. So comes senior year and three of the freshmen are excused from the final two weeks of indoor track to try out for baseball. I was really unhappy that that had not been an option for me. At least we finished first in the mile relay race that meet when I ran anchor."

"Did you ask if you could tryout after the end of track season?" Lynda asked.
"Apparently not. But my freshman year only Jerry left early to try out for baseball. I would have gone too if coach had not required me to stay for the rest of the indoor track season. Clearly, I did not know that trying out late was an option. Coach deliberately didn't tell me because he wanted me on his outdoor track relay team too. So now Jerry and I both get accepted at Grinnell

College. Jerry was a National Merit finalist, one of eleven in our graduating class of 859. I missed being a finalist by a few points but was more than good enough to get into Grinnell too. So now I refused to run track. The college track coach was known as killer and that did not appeal to me, but mostly we both wanted to play baseball. Baseball tryouts saw only twelve freshmen try for the freshman team, so we all were on the team. Problem was there was a shortage of coaches, so they had the last guy cut from the varsity team coach the freshmen team. He asked what position we played in high school, and it worked out so he had a relief pitcher and two of us on the bench, me and our Japanese exchange student. Grinnell is academically top notch, but not so good in most sports. So Akasuki and I watched from the bench as our team lost seven of the first seven games. Eighth and final game, top of the eighth inning behind seven to one, student coach sends Akasuki up to pinch hit. He swings mightily and tops the ball which rolls gently to the short stop who throws him out. He returns to our bench with a grin on his face touching both ears. So I was the only one who never got in any games. Sophomore year we both try out again, Jerry and I, not Akasuki and I, but now there are over twenty-four students from sophomore through senior. I was cut and Jerry was not, but since I had never played in a game in high school or freshman year, I don't believe they gave me a fair tryout. Had they had a

137

batting coach throw maybe three hundred pitches I believe I would have developed my timing and hit a few home runs, but of course we will never know for sure."

"Jerry told me one other thing I want to ask you about. Do you smoke pot?"
"Rarely now, but yes, I did and still occasionally do."
"He told me to ask you about the policeman story."
"He did, did he? Remember this was several years ago and will never happen again. A good friend of ours was a professional photographer. He was busy at that time, so I went to his studio after work to help him. We developed the pictures he had taken that day and hung them up to dry. While they dried, we lit up a joint or two. One night he was having problems with his girlfriend, and he smoked five or six joints. I stopped at four, I think. I drove home every night the same way and there was often a policeman watching for cars going through the red light or speeding on the nearly deserted streets.

"Knowing he was there, I carefully stopped at the light when it was yellow or red. That night I closed my eyes to rest them, and the light was still red when I opened them. Suddenly the police car was next to me with his lights flashing. He knocked on my window and I opened it. When the window was down, he asked me if I were drunk. I wasn't and said so. He looked over the inside of the car, asked me another thing or two and then he said 'young man, you have been sitting here for almost ten minutes. You pulled up and stopped at the red light. When it turned green you didn't move. It turned green three more times and still you sat there. May I escort you through the next green?'

I said, 'yes you may and thank you so much officer'. The light turned green, and he pulled out in the oncoming lane with his lights flashing. He looked to be blocking traffic on the cross street, but of course, there was none. He got out of his car and waved me across the street. I put my foot very softly on the gas and drove on home at no more than twenty miles an hour."

"You could have gone to jail."

"Perhaps, but I drove that road home many a night and he had seen me at that intersection many times about the same time of night. It was as if he knew me. He knew I was high on weed but he also knew I would get home safely. Drunk driving is illegal but being high on weed is a gray area. Besides I am white and most of the ones they arrest are black or brown."

"Is that really true?"

"Chicago area, yes, it is."

"It is likely true here too. Most crimes are committed by minorities."

Brad bit his lip and smiled through the pain of having actually bit his lip. One of his favorite charities was the NAACP. One of his favorite former girl friends had been brown. This was an argument he would not have with her.

Next Monday

The following Monday Brad told Jerry that he was going to discuss all sticking points with Lynda at dinner, things like dogs and children and travel. If all went as well as he expected it to, he would propose to her the following week.

At dinner that night, after sitting down and ordering a drink, Brad began by asking Lynda

"Do you have a number of children you would want to raise? After we are married of course."

"I think two would be ideal, one boy and one girl preferably. You?"

"Two or three. Are Mr. Cash and Furball enough, or would you like more pets? Or fewer pets?"

"I think two is plenty. More would require more time, more attention and more money."

"How do you feel about travel? Any favorite places? Anywhere you wouldn't want to go?"

"If we were married you said we would live in Oak Park. Right? So, my favorite trip would be to come back here to Piggott. Probably at least twice a year. After that New York, Glacier National Park, Paris, London, and Prague. Wherever you wanted, but not the Congo or anywhere where violence is commonplace. Is this quiz to see if we are compatible? After sleeping together for the past six weeks or so. You really are weird sometimes."

"Thank you for that. I hope you love weird because I do love you. Since we are in sync on nearly everything, I declare us ultra-compatible."

"Brad honey, I don't think we are ultra anything. Let's just eat and stare into each other's eyes for a while since the waiter is almost to our table with dinner."

"Over and out."

Back at the B&B while Lynda was in the kitchen with Millie Jerry asked Brad, "How did the compatibility quiz go?"

"Funny she used those very words. Did you forewarn her?"

"I'm sorry, yes I did. It just slipped out before I could stop myself. I doubt it did any harm. She knows you want to marry her; she loves you, no foul, no harm."

"My marriage is not quite basketball you know. I only plan to marry once, and I would rather be fully prepared going in and not be surprised afterwards."

"And now you are."

"And now I am."

A couple of days later Lynda asked Brad her questions. "Why do you always seem to be doing everything you possibly can for everyone else? Bringing Jerry here, cleaning Aunt Millie's house and doing your own bedding here, having had several Foster Children through Foster Parents Plan including two at one time, giving money to the Free and Charitable Clinics, going to the Hephzibah Children's Home to read to the orphans, buying used books to give to the Hemingway Foundation, picking up sticks on the lawn and salt on the carpet at Hemingway's Birth House, driving little old ladies home from the Nineteenth Century Club and or up to Petoskey, belonging to the Peace Action Club, writing letters for Amnesty International, letting your sister live in your house at less than two thirds of the market rate, taking your parents to dinner weekly when none of your siblings ever do, giving a dollar to every homeless person in Chicago, driving your older friends to your stamp clubs, loaning your new car to that nitwit from the School of Metaphysics who brought it back damaged and lied to you and said she didn't do it, and so on?"

"Wow, you remember everything I told you, don't you? You remember even a few things I didn't tell you. To answer generically, the more you give the more you will receive. Specifically, you know why Jerry. I would have walked barefoot to the tip of South America for him if he needed it. We are best friends and have been for more than twenty-five years. Why money, 'I was hungry, and you fed me not, thirsty and you gave me naught to drink, naked and you didn't cloth me."

"That is Jesus and yet you don't go to church or didn't before I asked you and Jerry to come with me."

"Jesus taught universal truths. I live in the universe. As far as money, I was taught to always give whenever and wherever you can. When I was seven years old and going to the Baptist Church with mom (dad worked Sundays so we rode two buses to get to church), I pledged ten cents a week in my offering envelopes. Needing candy money, I asked mom for a nickel and five pennies each week. She complied and I put seven cents in each envelope and spent three cents on penny candy. End of fiscal year my church statement read due thirty-six cents. Mom asked how that could be as that was not a multiple of a dime. I confessed, we paid up, and she scolded me so badly I never stole another penny again. I am still trying to erase that stain from my soul."
"You were seven years old. God forgave you immediately."
"What else? Oh, Hemingway. Ginie and Bill Cassin said they had two homes, theirs and Ernie's. I liked the sound of that so much I think of Hemingway's Birth House as my second home, too. You missed I have eight charities withdraw twenty, twenty-five, thirty, or forty dollars from my checking account the eighteenth of each month. As far as anything else, Jerry has a saying, 'Where there is a will there is a way, but if no Will is present Brad will do it."

"Jerry loves you as much as you love him. He is teasing you with affection."

"Of course. You know by now we tease each other as often as we are together. Maybe Hemingway wasn't his thing, and he collects stamps tepidly. Still, he became an Eagle Scout and I quit merit badges as a Star Scout, but we are as close as any two not gay men ever can be. Next question?"

"One more question. Tell me about Mary." Lynda flinched when she said that, and Brad knew she knew all about Mary already.

"Jerry told you to ask me that, too," Brad said. "I certainly wasn't going to mention her."

"It was not his fault. I made him tell me all about you so there will be no secrets in our relationship. I refused to start his massage until he told me the worst thing you had ever done. He said to ask you about Mary. He got his massage."

"Okay. Whole truth. Mary and I were two of the top programmers at our insurance company. There was a spot where we added live code directly before a critical branch. That was necessary because computers only read actual code and they can't make changes and recompile every day. Rather than recompile every day, we coded special one-time selection requests each day. Any mistake and the system crashed. So, one week she coded and I verified it was correct, next week we flipped and I coded and she verified. Thing is, we went into a conference room with two hours to get the job done and we finished in about eight minutes. The boss had no idea how smart we were. We then talked personal things for the rest of the two hours. After about six weeks she invited me to her apartment in Hyde Park, the very liberal part of Chicago by the University of Chicago. I went because her husband, an adjunct professor at the University was home and I didn't see any reason not to. We three drank Vodka. After one pitcher and lots of crackers and cheese her husband went into the kitchen to refill the pitcher with more vodka mix."

Brad paused to decide just what to say next. He had to tell the truth because Jerry had set him up. He had also promised Lynda he would never lie to her.

He continued, "I said I couldn't drink any more or I'd be too drunk to drive home. She laughed and kissed me on the lips. I knew we were very much attracted to each other, but I thought it couldn't go anywhere because she was married. Mark returned with the second pitcher. She told him I was spending the night. Instead of me sleeping on the couch as I had expected, she pulled me into the bedroom, and he said something like I'll sleep on the couch. She then said she loved me and undressed us both. With Mark's permission we made love both before and after we slept. In the morning I called in sick and she said tell them I am sick too. She might have been joking but that is what I said next."

"So, you committed adultery."

"It was nine years ago. I was inexperienced enough to want to see what being with someone who loves you was like. By that time fidelity seemed almost non-existent. Her husband asked me to sleep with her saying she was happy when with me and he wanted her to be happy. After a couple of months during which he seduced some five other women, Mary and I decided to go to Europe together. We planned it thoroughly, a month of travel, dining and drinking, sightseeing, and even attending a festival in Spain. Mark totally gave us his blessing. Four days before our vacation she backed out. Mark was a diabetic and was having some sort of diabetic fit. He needed her at home. I think he knew if the month went as we hoped we would be completely in love by the time we got home. He figured out the way to prevent her from going without saying he didn't want her to go. It was too late to cancel my plane ticket and I was going to see Europe for the first time, so I went alone. She wrote me a letter care of American Express in Madrid basically saying it is over and thanks for the memories."

"Didn't you see her at work when you got home?" Lynda asked.

"Actually, we both quit that job less than two weeks after I got home. Mary and Mark moved to the west coast and there was never any further contact. There was nothing left to be said. Any more questions?"

"That's it. Now I know you better than any other man I have ever known, and you are the only one I have ever known physically. Just don't ever tell me how many other women you have known because I really, really don't want to know."

"So it is and so it shall ever be."

"You weird, weird man. Why do I love you so much? That is not a question, don't answer."

After going back home, and after a second glass of wine, two kisses and three hugs, she knew she had to ask another question.

"Is it true you have been engaged three times?" Lynda asked as she set down her empty wine glass.

"Did Jerry tell you that too?"

"Do you always answer a question with a question? But yes, he told me that, too. I wasn't going to ask that, but after the Mary story I think it best I know about the others too."

"We will be up late, but if you really want to know, here goes."

When she just sat there looking at him, Brad knew she really wanted to know.

He began in chronological sequence. "The first one was my college girlfriend Michelle. She was the first girl who dated me for over a year. I spent spring break at her home in Saint Louis. Her parents were very conservative, and it turns out she was too, but mostly we agreed on the basics. We would cross the highway and study together at the church across from the college library. They left the church open so students could study there in a quiet place. About half the time we were alone, half the time another couple was there. After about ninety minutes of studying, we would kiss and hug about five minutes and then I would walk her back to her dorm. She had to be inside by midnight, and I had to be back on the men's side of the railroad track within minutes of midnight.

"Because she was a year behind me, I felt I had to propose before I graduated to guarantee she would remain in my life. She said yes and I was elated. Then about two weeks before I was to graduate, she got a letter from her parents telling her not to engage in petting and other sexual stimulation until after she was married. I laughed saying they are about six months late with that advice, but it upset her so much she told me the engagement was off. We went back and forth the next two weeks between being in love and being broken up. Finally, the night before I was to graduate, I realized it really was over in twenty-four hours. Without thinking as she went up the stairs inside her dorm, I smashed the window in the door with my right fist. By the time I got back to my dorm I had lost a lot of blood, so the dorm captain called the college nurse and I walked over there alone with my hand wrapped in a hand towel. The nurse stopped the bleeding, or maybe the towel did, the thumb and wrist were bandaged up and I went home to lay awake all night processing the day and evening. Next day she held my hand as we walked to the gym for the graduation ceremony, but she dropped it quickly saying she didn't want to hurt me. My hand didn't hurt as much as my mind, but I decided not to say that. When the college president gave me my diploma and shook my hand was when I felt a sharp pain in my hand, but I knew it was my own fault and did not grimace or show him in any way just how much pain that handshake caused me. Six months later I realized she was not at all compatible with me and I thanked her in my mind for seeing that before I did. Another glass of wine?"

"No thanks."

"I need another one before I go on. Actually, I think I'll have a cold beer now."

Back with a stein of cold beer Brad resumed the story he wished he didn't have to tell.

"The second one was much more real than the first. It was with Alice. I guess that was the most real one before you. I met her at a church party. She didn't want to be there, but because she missed the morning service her father required her to attend the young people's party that Sunday night. We skipped out soon after we met and after getting something to eat, we went back to my Condo. By the time I drove her home I thought of her as my girlfriend and she seemed to be falling in love with me, too. We dated for three years, and I was often at her parents' home. She still lived at home with her parents. Her family totally accepted me as a member of the family. At my parents' house she called my parents papa number two and mother number two. We travelled to several national parks together and even flew to Georgia together where we almost bought a lot on a man-made lake. Everyone expected us to get married and I proposed to her sometime near the three-year mark. She was all excited and her father reserved the church for a Saturday in July, he bought her a wedding dress, I bought her an engagement ring, we had almost decided on invitations, and then she looked me in the eye one Sunday night and ordered me to tell her I loved her. I did love her but am not one to take orders lightly, so I replied something unbelievably stupid like 'What am I? A puppet who says everything I am told to say?'

"It seems her ex-boyfriend had reappeared, and she wanted to decide what to do about that. My stupid, not correct answer sent her into his bed and that was all she wrote. Cancel the church, put the dress in storage, give me the ring back and move in with him. I think that happened so that I would be free to find you. She already has a son with him and another on the way, and I have been forgotten. However, her parents remained friendly with me and to this day her father tells her what I am doing, and he tells me a little bit about what she is doing. Since I have been here in Piggott, I haven't heard anything from him, of course. And I haven't thought of her until tonight when you asked me about my past engagements."

"But you were really in love with her?"
"I believed so, but you must believe me it was nothing like what I feel for you. She was a terrific person, but you are my soul mate, the one person I was meant to find and love unconditionally."
"And the third engagement?"
"It is late. Do you want to stay up all night?"
"If that is what it takes."
"Let me start by saying some people are sincere and some play games. The third time was not sincere. I worked with a very well-built young lady when I worked at a different insurance company. My job at that time was teaching programming. I loved it because I taught a class and went home with no worry of a night call about a computer problem. Halfway through the

class I was told that graduating students were baffled by needing to modify code someone else had written. So, I found a program I had been asked to modify the year before. It was easy for me and met the criteria of needing to add code into an existing program. It required three different places with some new code. To my surprise the entire class were upset at how hard it was. My boss said to let them work in teams and I said sure. Only half as many programs for me to grade.

"Well, this well-built girl was one of my students. I talked to her a fair amount about the assignment without giving her any direct help. That Friday after work Jerry and I were meeting for dinner. I think he called me while I was talking to her or something and suddenly, she was coming with me to meet Jerry. I was determined not to give her any advantage in the assignment, and it never came up. After dinner she invited us back to her apartment. We went and an hour later Jerry was sleeping on her couch and she and I were in her bed upstairs. You know this is not normal, but men don't often say no to sex when they are not in a serious relationship. Go with the flow. Next night she and I had a dinner date and ended up at my house and she spent the night. Five workdays that next week and each night she came home with me, and we had sex every night. The best sex of my life before I met you was with her.

"After eight nights in a row in the sack she said something like 'my best friend asked if you were going to marry me. I told her you hadn't asked me.' Clearly, she was playing a game, but to keep up the sex I asked her to marry me the next night. She accepted, of course, and I found Alice's ring and gave it to her. She came over to meet my parents. Mom couldn't believe we were engaged in like ten days of dating, but she assured mom it was real. Then she went home to see her mother and did not wear the ring and told her nothing about me except only that we were dating. When she told me she thought she was pregnant it became clear to me. Her mother's boyfriend had raped her, and she needed a man to marry if she were pregnant. If I had gotten her pregnant it wouldn't have showed up for at least another six weeks. We then began to spend only one night a week together and when she found out she wasn't pregnant she gave me back the ring. She had started dating someone else and said she was doing it for me so she would be more mature when we got married. Funny sidebar here. One day she told me she had gone into the lady's room and the ring was too big for her finger and it flew across the room when she waved her hand. She asked a lady in the end stall if she had seen a diamond ring fly past. Thank goodness she found it as I had spent well over twelve hundred dollars on it."

"So, you played along with her just for the sex."

"You could say that. I have no idea what would have happened if she had been pregnant. We both would have loved to have a baby, but she wasn't the right one for me to marry. I hope I would have told her so and broken it off with her in any case. To my astonishment she called me when she quit dating the other guy and said I could call her again. Since she had quit the job after the intro class was over, I never called and never saw her again."

"So, I am to be number four in the long line of your engagements."

"Actually, you will always be number one in my heart and the only marriage I really want to have happen. Everything I have done and learned has led me to you."

"Millie is up now. Let's have coffee and not tell her we were talking all night long."

"Mum's the word," Brad said, but his large yawn made the words mumbled. He almost fell asleep washing pans that afternoon, and he promised himself no more all-nighters when the next day is a workday.

155

Say it isn't So

Friday Lynda wasn't feeling well and decided to call in sick. The other server at the café was at work so she was told to take it easy, get some sleep and come in tomorrow. Brad finished cleaning the house, kissed Lynda on the lips, her cold be damned, and walked to work. There were lots of pots to wash due to a very good day of business and he set out to walk home about ten minutes later than usual. He decided to walk the long way home and go past the Hemingway-Pfeiffer Museum. His friend Sue from the bookstore was just leaving so he talked to her for twenty minutes. When he got home, he was about forty minutes late. Lynda clearly had been crying.

"Sit down," she ordered him.
He sat down but noticed she was still standing and holding Jerry's hand.
"What's wrong? Are you still sick?"
"No. I just have a cold. Oh God. Oh God, I can't do it."
Jerry squeezed her hand and put his arm around her. "Take your time. It'll be okay."
Two minutes passed but it seemed like an hour to each of them. Had she wrecked his car? Had she found out she was pregnant? Had Aunt Millie died? What could possibly be so emotional?
Lynda finally was composed enough to talk.

"I love you Brad. You know that. And I always will. But today I realized I love Jerry too. I was giving him a massage and he looked up at me, gently pulled me down on top of him, and kissed me."

"We both love him. He is our best friend."

"No. I am *in* love with him. I felt something in that kiss that I don't feel with you. You are my best friend and Jerry is the man I love and want to marry."

Brad looked down. Silence. Did he hear what he had heard? Did she mean what she had said? Should he stay and talk or get up and run out?

"I'm so, so sorry. I never meant to hurt you. I never meant for this to happen. We both have been crying for over an hour. Please be okay. Please, please, please."

Brad knew what he had to say. "I am okay. I hurt like I never wanted to hurt, but I have a great tolerance for pain. This will pass. You are still my best friends. I need for you both to be happy. It is because of me you are both happy. And just as Jerry came back from the brink, I will come back someday too. For now, I need to go for a long walk. I need to be alone. No actually I need Mr. Cash to walk with me. God Bless you and keep you."

As he got Mr. Cash's leash Lynda said softly, "Not necessary to say the benediction."

Brad and Mr. Cash walked for over an hour and when they came home Brad decided to lay down on the couch to spend the night. Mr. Cash went into the bedroom and saw their bed was empty and returned to sleep on the couch too. Lynda was in Jerry's bed.

Two days later they had the serious talk needed but not possible immediately after the announcement. They went to the bench across from the Hemingway-Pfeiffer House, held hands for a short while, and then Lynda began to try and make things right. "You know Jerry is going to ask you to be the best man at our wedding."

"I expect he will." Brad said. After about twenty seconds he added, "I will do it, of course."

"You know that we both love you. We want you to be living with us, at least at first. You will be the Godfather of our first child. I think Jerry will name our first son Bradley Miller Goddard, after you and your hero Hemingway."

"I'm honored. We both are. Both Ernie and me."

"Don't be sarcastic. Hurting you is the most horrible thing I have ever done. A week ago, I was expecting to marry you. Now I want you to try to understand I don't love you any less, I just love Jerry more."

"I do understand, and I applaud you for having the courage to do what you had to do. You must live your life your way and this was the only decision you could make. My happiness is my problem, your happiness is your call and you called it totally right. It is like Hemingway in the Spanish Civil War. You remember he drove an ambulance in Italy in World War One and came to love the Italians. When he was severely wounded in the front-line trench, he managed to drag the surviving Italian across a field to safety."

"I thought he carried him on his back?"

"His friend Ted Brumback wrote that in a letter to Ernie's parents, but I believe with 247 pieces of shrapnel in his leg he was lucky he could even walk. Then as he crossed the field toward safety, he was shot in the knee just behind his kneecap which was displaced. After that it was impossible to carry anyone on his back. I think he dragged the wounded soldier across the field. But my point here is he loved the Italians. When the fascists went to help Franco in the Spanish Civil War, Ernest went to Madrid and helped the Spanish fight against the Italian soldiers. See what I am saying? He loved the Italians and hard as it was for him, he helped the Spanish kill the Italians. He did what he believed was right, weird as it felt to him. Same as what you did. It couldn't be, except it had to be."

"You have a story for everything, and they all involve Hemingway."

"Almost true. Here is one not involving him. Also, in World War One Christmas Day 1914. Germans were singing Christmas Carols in their trenches. So were the British in their trenches on the other side of the field. When the British sang *Oh Come all ye Faithful*, the

Germans started singing *Adeste Fideles*. Same hymn, different language. Then thousands of soldiers came out of their trenches, met in the middle, a few hugged their enemies, they exchanged gifts like cigarettes or whatever they had, and for one day there was a truce. They all knew wonderful as that event was, soon they would return to killing each other. They had to. It was their destiny. They were soldiers."

"So, you forgive me, but soon we will be at war?"

"No! My point is you have to do what you have to do. Make your choice and don't second guess yourself. Create your life as you want it, not as Aunt Millie wants it, not as I want it, not as Jerry wants it, but solely as you want it."

Brad knew he had to get in another Hemingway story that seemed to fit in. Somehow talking seemed to blunt the overwhelming numb pain he had been feeling.

"In World War Two Ernie fought the Germans in France as a reporter who was right there with the action. When German soldiers retreated into Germany to make a strong stand at their border, they moved so quickly that a large number of soldiers were left behind. Those men would try to get back to Germany on their own. French snipers would often shoot them as they walked past. Ernie wrote about that in *Black Ass at the Crossroads*. The narrator shoots a very young German, probably only sixteen or seventeen years old. They drag him off the road and see he is dying. The narrator feels a sympathy for the kid and tells his partner to hold the kid's hand and comfort him until he dies so he won't have to die alone. Same point, he had compassion for the kid but had to kill him because he was at war with the country the kid was fighting for. He couldn't let compassion overrule the choice he had to make."

"Thank you for trying to understand. And be sure my choice doesn't involve anyone dying. I couldn't take it if anything happened to you. Promise me!"

"You have my word. I promise. Mr. Cash and I will arrive safely in Oak Park not long after you two do."

"Thank you."

She hugged him for about thirty seconds and their time as a couple was officially over.

The Wedding

Lynda went to work the day after the big reveal. Brad and Jerry ate lunch at the café as always, they walked back home as always, and fewer than twenty words had been said between them in all that time. Jerry went into the kitchen, Brad put on his grubbies and walked back to wash pots and pans and if possible, to wash away his empty feeling. He wasn't sure you could wash a hollow empty gut with anything but time, but he scrubbed each pan as hard as he could and thought the disappearing food was a substitute for his love for Lynda. When he got home, he joined Jerry, Millie and Lynda in the kitchen and said a bit too spritely,

"Let's start planning your wedding."

"Thank you for offering to help," Jerry said.

He sounded as if he had been caught by surprise.

After a few moments of thought Jerry said, "You can drive me to the Jewelry store tomorrow to pick out a ring. Lynda is going to have her mother help with most everything else. Wedding at her church. Her mom will get out her own wedding dress and resew it to fit Lynda. You can think about something borrowed. She has a beautiful blue ring to wear. The wedding dress is old. Something new will be the garter which I'll remove and toss to the guys. I hope you catch it. Damn it Brad, we need to go from two to four, not two to three."

"You know I already picked out a ring which seemed perfect to me," Brad said.

"All you have to do is pick it up and make the payment. On something borrowed, how about I loan her a hundred-dollar bill and you two pay me back when you are both working? If I am paid back, it will have been borrowed."

"How about she borrows something from her mother, and you be my best man. You have a little over two weeks to think of a toast. I know you are good with words Mr. Novelist."

"About that, you win the dollar bet we made, but gradually my novel is going to emerge from my muddled brain."

"I know. And we will be eager to read it when it does see the light of day."

Millie did not much like Brad and Mr. Cash sleeping on the couch in the common room, but she completely understood why Brad wanted it to be that way. She could not imagine how she would have felt if her late husband had come home with one of her friends and had relations on their bed. She started to hug Brad each night as he went into the washroom to get ready for bed and before she left to read in her bedroom. She hoped that might easy his pain a little bit.

Two weeks to plan a wedding is not a long time but things were resolved quickly. Jerry's mother would drive down two days before the wedding and pay for the rehearsal dinner. She would also loan the bride her silver necklace which had been in the family for over one hundred years. The café would cater the wedding dinner in the church gymnasium. Jerry loved the ring Brad had reserved and paid for it and gave it to Lynda. She showed it to everyone she knew to show them her engagement was now a reality. Brad had both his and Jerry's suits dry-cleaned. Lynda's mother sewed two full days and her wedding dress now fit Lynda perfectly. Invitations were printed at the local quick print store and mailed to twenty-four invited guests. In the church bulletin the Sunday before the wedding every member of the church was invited to attend. The bride and groom would leave town in Lynda's car, so it was washed, and decorations made to attach to the back bumper the morning of the wedding. Brad offered to drink a lot of canned beer so there would be enough cans for the car to drag. The car gas tank was filled to the top.

Jerry and Lynda packed two suitcases each to take with them to Oak Park. Lynda identified a few pieces of furniture her parents would ship up in two weeks or so so they would arrive after the couple returned from their honeymoon. Brad called his sister and found out she had just closed on her townhouse. She would move in on

Jerry and Lynda's wedding day. They agreed he would stay in her townhouse the first couple of weeks back home so Jerry and Lynda could live in his and Jerry's house and he wouldn't be in their way. He pointed out that he had put the house in a living trust and Jerry was the first trustee after him. All Jerry had to do was make the mortgage payments and he and Lynda would own the house in twenty-three years. Brad pointed out Jerry was a co-owner already. He had helped paint the house inside and out. He had bought the bed in the guest room where he slept most nights, and it was now his room. Much of the food in the pantry was his. He had a key to the house. If anything happened to Brad, he would be the trustee and the trust would still own the house. If things went well for the newlyweds they could repay Brad some part of his equity in the house, but that was flexible and any small check would do each month or every other month, whichever they found easier. Brad would remove his name from the trust, and Jerry would be trustee and Lynda would be first trustee in reserve. Ironically Brad's name would no longer appear on the Bradley O. Trust #101.

One week before the wedding Jerry confessed to Brad, "I started to have feelings for Lynda about a month after we arrived here. Because I knew you had them too, I tried to hide my feelings. I wanted you two to marry and live happily ever after because of what you did for me.

166

Then one day she looked me in the eyes, and I knew she was very attracted to me too. I kissed her to see what would happen and she melted into my arms. We both felt terrible for a few days but decided that she loved me more than she loved you and it would be a mistake to throw away our happiness in order to not hurt you. We hid our feelings three straight nights and knew we had to tell you that night. It is my sincere hope and prayer that you find someone else to love and the four of us can be together constantly. Until that happens, I think you can agree we will be unable to all live together."

"I do agree. You two need months to learn how best to live together as a married couple. No one else should be there to be in the way. I will stay at my sister's townhouse for a month or two while I decide where best to live on my own. I am thinking condo again, but it is too soon to decide that."

Later that day Lynda also felt the need to explain more to Brad. "You told me once that you were in love with two women at the same time. It tears at you every minute. How long can this continue. Is it possible to not hurt either of them? Probably not. Which one do you hurt? Probably both of them. After that day there is no turning back. You postpone deciding for another day. So, I was massaging Jerry's leg, which I was thinking didn't really need it any longer, and I paused and looked down at him. He looked up at me with a longing such as

I had never seen before except with you, and then he gently put his arms around me and pulled me down on top of him. At that moment I had to decide which of you to choose. He decided for me in a way by kissing me, long and gently for what seemed more than a minute. Then he took my hand and placed it on his penis. It was already hard and as I continued to wonder what to do his underwear came off and after that so did mine. He was making it clear that he was in love with me, too. I just went along with him without doing much and then he was inside of me. It felt about the same as with you until just before he came when I felt as if a controlled bolt of electricity went from him into me. I had never felt that before and I knew in that instant that I had chosen him by letting him choose me. We lay there whispering I love you to each other and then as in terror, how are we going to tell Brad. I called in sick the next morning and we rehearsed how to tell you without losing your love for us. Finally, we just cried ourselves to sleep because we hadn't slept even one minute all the night before. You must know if there had been a way to not hurt you, we would have done anything to find it, but there was no way. Please believe me I love you no less than before. I just love Jerry more, more than I thought possible before I met the two of you. Please forgive us and wish us all good things. You will always be our best friend. Always and forever."

"Your happiness will be enough for me," he replied. They both knew he was lying.

"Just focus on your wedding now." Brad said.

"I feel like the soldier in *All Quiet on the Western Front.* He has been shot and will bleed to death, but he holds the letter he just received from his lover. But as he begins to read her last message the letter slips from his hand and floats slowly away from his outstretched hand and disappears down river as he closes his eyes for the last time. But no worry, I am not dying, and I will find a way back from the abyss. And the happier you two are the easier that will be for me. Thank you for telling me that. Hearing it from you is the first step for me on the climb back up."

Brad kissed her softly on the cheek and left the room angry at himself for crying yet again.

The rehearsal dinner went well, and Jerry's mother made friends with Lynda's parents and Millie. They would take turns having the kids on holidays. Oak Park for Thanksgiving and Piggott for Christmas.

The morning of the wedding the sun shone, and the temperature was 73 degrees Fahrenheit. Brad and Jerry walked over to the church. Millie and the three parents drove over together. Lynda drove over with her bridesmaids Lauren and Loren. The church filled up by ten minutes before ten with everyone who was coming.

Daisies, hydrangeas, gardenias, baby's breath, and ranunculus were tied to the end of each pew and stood in tall flowerpots on short dark brown tables on each side of the alter.

At ten Lynda's brother Billy escorted his mother to her seat up front on the left side. Then the other usher, Loren's boyfriend, escorted Jerry's mother to her seat up front on the right side. Brad, as best man, stood to the right of Reverend Hegel and soon Billy and Loren's boyfriend took their places next to him. All three wore crisp pressed dark suits with tan ties. Reverend Hegel's six-year-old daughter came down the aisle next and threw rose petals on the aisle and a few stray petals onto people's laps. She seemed to be stealing the show but not too far behind her came the bridesmaids. They were dressed in identical coral dresses which matched hers. Loren and Lauren walked in lock step and looked only straight ahead. After they took their places opposite the ushers the music stopped.

Two minutes of silence seemed about a half hour to the people sitting in the pews. Each one turned discretely to look to the open door where the bride would soon appear. When Wagner's Bridal Chorus shouted from the organ and filled every nook of the sanctuary, everyone stood up virtually in unison and looked to the doorway. Another minute passed and then Lynda entered wearing her mother's resized wedding dress in pure white. Her father smiled slightly as she held his arm and walked slowly up to the group at the altar. The music stopped and the service began. It was nearly identical to every other Protestant wedding for everyone present except Jerry who suddenly felt his legs going weak, Brad who felt the pit of his stomach fall at least thirty feet, and Lynda who felt like she was in a play on a stage and wasn't playing herself. They read the vows they had written which had been approved by Reverend Hegel, exchanged rings, were introduced as Mr. and Mrs. Goddard, shared their first kiss as a married couple, and walked out to a spirited version of Beethoven's *Ode to Joy*.

Everyone passed the receiving line, said congratulations, kissed the bride on the cheek and shook the groom's hand before going into the gym for the dinner. There were name cards at each place along with a small bag of candy. Everyone was seated at the place reserved for them by the name card Lynda had written by hand. Brad wasn't too comfortable having to give the toast, but he was required to do so as best man. Seeing that everyone had a glass of champagne he stood up and tapped his glass with his spoon to get everyone's attention. Nervously Jerry leaned over and kissed Lynda as he had to do each time someone tinkled their champagne glass.

Brad cleared his throat and began, "I would like to propose a toast to Jerry and Lynda. I'm Bradley Hull. I'm sure you all know me as Jerry's best friend and best man, but if you don't, well done on sneaking into the wedding unnoticed! All of us gathered together in this room, we've got something really important in common – none of us have got a clue what I'm going to say next. I want to start by saying that, of all the weddings I've attended over the years, this one is, by far, the most recent. Jerry and Lynda are kind, intelligent, gorgeous, charming…," looking directly at them, "Sorry, I'm having trouble reading your writing Jerry, you'll have to tell me the rest later.

"Jerry has been my best friend for more than twenty-five years, so I tell you from experience that he has all the virtues I dislike and none of the vices I admire. Lynda is the most charming, funny, intelligent woman I have ever met and therefore the first and only one good enough to marry Jerry. I ask you to raise a glass to my two best friends and join me in congratulating them on their marriage and wishing them all the best always; health, wealth, beautiful children, funny loving pets, educational travel, a full library, dozens of great friends, more than dozens actually, laughter every day, supportive families, and the willingness to tolerate me now and again. To Lynda and Jerry."

After most guests took a sip of champagne, Brad added, "The food is self-serve so the head table will go first, then table 1, table 2, and so on. Hopefully when table 9 goes up there will still be something good left to eat."

Brad sat down and drank the rest of his champagne, waited for the rest of the head table to go up, and when Jerry and Lynda sat down with their meal he went up and joined the guests from table 1 in the line. He wasn't hungry.

Millie Talk

The morning after Jerry and Lynda had left on their drive to Oak Park Brad was forty minutes late for breakfast. Millie served him black coffee, pancakes with butter and maple syrup, a glass of orange juice and a small bowl of fruit. She then sat down opposite him at the table with her own cup of coffee.

"You know you are not the only one at this table who is feeling a deep sense of loss," she said.

"My favorite niece has visited me at least once a week her entire life except when she was traveling. Then she sent post cards daily, or more recently called or texted me nearly every day. I will miss her as much as you will. More actually because after you go back to work you will start seeing Jerry regularly, maybe not the first month or so, but it will come. And she will be there too, and they will remain your best friends."

She paused and drank a few sips of her coffee. "Not only that, but you have been the son I always wanted. You have done everything you could possibly do to help me. You have kept my house even cleaner than I kept it. You improved my garden. You brought Mr. Cash into my life, and I learned to love a dog as much as I loved Furball. And Jerry. We three supported him and watched him blossom into the terrific young man he used to be before his accident. So, realize you lost the marriage you wanted, but I am losing all three of you. It will be so quiet here, so lonesome, so empty."

Brad processed what he had heard and then said, "You are right. Forgive me for being selfish this past couple of weeks. You know I will keep in touch with you, and so will they."

"I certainly expect you to. Are you still hungry? I've got lots more pancake batter, more fruit, cereal."

"No thanks. The first day after she told me I couldn't eat a thing. At least now I am eating almost normal meals."

"You will be fine. You are a strong person. You are a kind person. You work very hard. You always try to do the right thing. So, when are you leaving? Tomorrow?"

"Yes. I will pack today, say goodbye to the people at the Hemingway-Pfeiffer Museum, fill my car with gas, get cash at the bank to settle up with you, and go to bed earlyish."

"So, breakfast tomorrow at seven? "Millie asked.

"Fine. I'll be on the road at eight and home before noon Wednesday."

"Home?"

"Well okay, not our old house. Jerry and Lynda will be living there. I will be staying with my sister in her new townhouse. I think Jerry and Lynda will buy out my share of the house and I'll find a townhouse for Mr.

Cash and me. They need much more room than I do, and Jerry and I agreed we shouldn't live together ever again now that he is married."

"I thought you didn't live together before."

"Technically we didn't until last year when he moved the rest of his things from his mother's house, but before that he spent about four nights a month at his mother's house and the rest of the time with me. He had his own room and kept most of his clothes and books there. He is probably there now or will be when they return from their honeymoon. They will turn my room into an office and computer room. I expect to find whatever I didn't put in storage when we came here will be boxed up and waiting for me by the front door."

After a long pause he added, "Aunt Millie, I thank you from the bottom of my heart for your letting us have a room for six months, for all you did for us, for being a third mother to me. I love you almost as much as I love my own mother."

Millie got up and hugged Brad for more than a minute. She was not crying but tears did run down his face.

"I am getting older and running a B&B is a lot of work" she said. "If you want to get away from them and come down here to work with me, I will welcome you. I can't pay you what you make in Chicago, but you would live and eat for free here so your salary could go directly into the bank. You can volunteer at the Hemingway-Pfeiffer

Museum. Their tour guides receive a small salary from the university, and you will have enough vacation to attend all the Hemingway Conferences you want to. Who knows, someday you might own the B&B. Think about my offer whenever you get the Black Ass."

"The Black Ass! Shows you have been listening to me talk about Ernie."

"Yes, I have, and since you two came here I have read three of his books. *The Sun Also Rises, For Whom the Bell Tolls*, and *A Farewell to Arms."*

"Three of his best."

Millie continued, "Some people around here don't care for him because of the way he treated Pauline. But I recognize he is a great writer and I see such admiration in your voice when you talk about him that I have come to admire him, too. If you will stay here with me, we can have talks here about Hemingway's stories. I think several of my friends will read him and attend, and probably Laurie with an 'au.' I know Lorey with an 'o' is not too fond of you, but I think from what Laurie with an 'au' has said to me she could easily become your girlfriend. She does like you but wouldn't say or do anything as long as Lynda was with you. When she talked about the trip the four of you took to the Dean B. Ellis Library, she decided that Jerry was clearly not for her and wished she could trade boyfriends with Lynda.

She would love to hear from you now. So, what do you say to my offer? Do you want to be an Inn keeper?"

"Not now, but I will keep it in mind."

They hugged for another couple of minutes before going to their separate bedrooms. Before he got the bedroom door shut Millie added,

"Brad, will you stay here with me for another week? I am worried you are not in the correct frame of mind to drive alone all the way to Oak Park. I keep thinking about how upset Jerry was before he drove into a tree. I couldn't live with myself if I let you repeat that accident. I won't charge you anything and you can touch up the paint on the back steps for me. Neither of us should be alone just yet. Another week should help us both. Please stay."

Brad stood in the doorway for about a half minute clearly thinking it over and then he said, "Of course I'll stay. They will be on their honeymoon that week getting used to being together and I would be with my sister who is still settling into her new townhouse. Thank you for helping avoid the raw emotions that would gnaw at me in Oak Park. Breakfast at eight?"

"Breakfast at eight."

The Direction You Go

Brad spent the week talking to Millie, touch up painting the steps, visiting the Hemingway-Pfeiffer Museum twice more, and reading Hemingway short stories. With no guests and no pressure both he and Millie began to return to their usual selves. They chose not to mention Lynda or Jerry at all. They went to the grocery store together and planned menus to please themselves as they were the only ones at dinner. Brad tried to remember the quotes he had used six months earlier and they both laughed at a few of them. The first guest booking at the B&B was scheduled for the ninth day after Brad had planned to leave, so he stayed yet one more day past the agreed on extra week. He repacked his car that night to be ready to leave shortly after breakfast.

He left the next day, ten days after Jerry and Lynda had left. Passing through the laundry area he said good-bye to Colonel Schmidt, gave him his freedom and wished him a wonderful time at Oktoberfest. As he drove toward the highway he waved good-bye to the Hemingway-Pfeiffer Museum which was only a few blocks out of his way. Once on the road out of Piggott he spoke to Mr. JR Cash, "Well Buddy, guess you are with me for the long haul, and we will have to learn to live away from Jerry and Lynda. We'll both miss them dearly, but at least we have each other."

Mr. JR Cash was riding in the passenger seat even though Brad knew it would have been safer for him to ride in the back seat. JR put his front paws on Brad's leg and licked his hand which Brad knew should be on the steering wheel, but which was slowly and gently scratching Mr. JR. He drove slowly north on I-55, having chosen that route because it was not the route he and Jerry had come south on. Cars whizzed past at 75 or 85 miles an hour and they often looked askance at him doing just under 65. Two male drivers gave him the finger. Because of Mr. Cash he had packed his meals and enough food for Mr. Cash for two or three days. They stopped at a rest area to walk, drink something, and eat one part of the first meal as a late-morning snack. The sun was shining but Brad felt as if he were driving through a heavy fog, no desire to get to his destination, no desire to think about what would come next, no smiles or laughter usually found on his road trips, no singing or music, no CD playing his favorite songs.

Remembering he had used jokes to help Jerry heal he searched his memory for some to make himself laugh. A hog farmer came into the church office. He told the receptionist he wanted to speak to the head hog at the trough. The receptionist told him you can't call the pastor the head hog at the trough. That is unacceptable. The farmer repeated I need to talk to the head hog at the trough. The receptionist repeated you can't talk that way about our pastor. Too bad the farmer said. I've had a good year and I came here to make a $10,000 donation to the church. The receptionist jumped up, went to the door of the pastor's office, opened it, and said, 'Hey hog-head, there is someone here to see you.'

Brad thought hard about a second joke he had recently heard. Scrunched knot, no, frayed knot, yes. Got it. A rope walked into a bar. I'd like a beer he said. Get out of here, we don't serve ropes here. He left and walked into a second bar down the block. I'd like a beer he said. Aren't you a rope? Well yes, I am. Please leave now, we don't serve ropes here. Frustrated outside the bar the rope took the various strands at the top of his head and pulled them down. Now he looked so droopy he tied the loose ends in a bun at the back of his head. In the third bar the bartender asked aren't you a rope. His reply, 'I am afraid not.'

What do you get when you mate an Elephant and a Rhinoceros? El if I no.
Two tickets, bring a friend if you have one. Can't possibly attend first night, second night if there is one. Unexpectedly a quote popped up in his head which

made him laugh because it wasn't really funny. David Berman said, 'I am the trick my mother played on the world.'

Why don't you ever see a blind parachutist? Because it scares the shit out of the seeing eye dog.
There was an opera singer in Oak Park who made the entire room laugh. He said he was invited to sing to a group of dementia patients. The best way to reach them is through music. First song was 'Try to remember the kind of September ...'
Thinking it couldn't be any worse, he agreed to sing to a room full of homeless people. First song from the Music Man was 'On the street where you live.' By now Brad had laughed three times and smiled two or three more times.

That made Brad start singing,
"I sing because I'm happy, I sing because I'm free
His eye is on the sparrow, and I know he watches me.
I sing because I'm happy, I sing because I'm free
I sing because my Savior has died on Calvary
I sing because I'm happy, I sing because I'm free
I sing because my buddy JR is next to me
I sing because I'm happy, I sing because I'm free
I sing because this interstate I drive no charge to me
I sing because I'm happy, I sing because I'm free
I sing because my singing supersedes my misery

I sing because I'm happy, I sing because I'm free
I sing because the birds I pass are singing back to me."

Now after laughing at jokes and singing out loud Brad decided he was ready to play his favorite Johnny Cash CD. He pulled over and stopped on the shoulder just long enough to get the CD out and put it into the player below his dashboard. By the third song he was singing along softly
'I forgot to remember to forget her.'

Just at that moment he saw the sign on the side of the road. It read Interstate Route 70 22 miles. He remembered that there was an ongoing writing class in Boulder, Colorado. If things were different, he would go there now and write his novel. Twenty-five minutes later they came to the exit to West I70 and his car drove right onto the exit ramp. He smiled and never gave a thought of turning back.
"You're going to love Boulder, JR."
JR perked up and licked his face. Brad knew he was saying 'We both will.' Together they sang along with Johnny *Sunday morning coming down.*

Brad turned off the CD and sang it again A cappella, sang it again, and then said very softly almost like a fading song,
"something   lost   somehow

something   lost   somehow
something   lost
something
lost
some   thing
lost
some   how.

disappearing
dis   appearing
dis   appear   ing
dream
disappearing   dream
a
long

a
long
gone
by
the
way."

"gone"

ACKNOWLEDGMENTS

I would like to thank the following for reading my work in progress and making valuable suggestions: My wife Karen Glass, my brother and his wife Carl and Sherry Glass, my sister and her husband Louise and Mike Forbes. I also want to thank Pam Lyons for offering to read and repair my spelling and my punctuation. Her notes helped a great deal.

I also want to thank Karen for formatting the book and for creating the cover mostly as I requested. She also assisted me in uploading everything to the printer.

David Berner, a former writer-in-residence at the Ernest Hemingway Birth House, was very helpful in teaching me self-publishing. He also replied to my inquiry and got me well on the way to self-publishing this novel. A published writer, his help was very valuable.

I began this novel in 1989 in Boulder, Colorado but put it aside in 1990 when I returned to Oak Park. A note from Anne Starkey Case, the first woman I was engaged to, got me back to working on it again in 2019. I began over from scratch but kept the same basic ideas as I had in the incomplete Colorado version.

All proceeds from sales of this novel will be donated to the Ernest Hemingway Foundation of Oak Park, hopefully to build a writing center behind the restored birth house. For that reason, I hope to sell more than a few copies. A total sale of 72,222 will cover the construction costs, or nearly so.

Every time I proofread the novel; I sing aloud the songs referred to. I recommend you do the same to enhance the reading experience. Words are available on the internet. You are not required to sing on key.

Sunday Morning Coming Down by Kris Kristofferson as sung by Johnny Cash

His Eye is on the Sparrow Olde Church Hymn

I Call Him by Johnny Cash

That's where my money goes Old English folk song

I forgot to remember to forget her by Johnny Cash

And the rest.